IN DEBT TO THE COWBOY

MILLER BROTHERS OF TEXAS BOOK TWO

NATALIE DEAN

Copyright © 2020, 2021, 2022, 2023 by Natalie Dean

ISBN: 978-1-964875-08-8

All rights reserved.

No part of this publication may be reproduced, distributed, or transmitted in any form or by any means, including photocopying, recording, or other electronic or mechanical methods, without the prior written permission of the publisher, except as permitted by U.S. copyright law. For permission requests, contact [include publisher/author contact info].

The story, all names, characters, and incidents portrayed in this production are fictitious. No identification with actual persons (living or deceased), places, buildings, and products is intended or should be inferred.

DEDICATION

I'd like to dedicate this book to YOU! The readers of my books. Without your interest in reading these heartwarming stories of love, I wouldn't have made it this far. So thank you so much for taking the time to read any and hopefully all of my books.

And I can't leave out my wonderful mother, son, sister, and Auntie. I love you all, and thank you for helping me make this happen.

Most of all, I thank God for blessing me on this endeavor.

OTHER BOOKS BY NATALIE DEAN

CONTEMPORARY ROMANCE

Miller Family Saga

BROTHERS OF MILLER RANCH
Miller Family Saga Series 1
Her Second Chance Cowboy

Saving Her Cowboy

Her Rival Cowboy

Her Fake-Fiance Cowboy Protector

Taming Her Cowboy Billionaire

Brothers of Miller Ranch Complete Collection

MILLER BROTHERS OF TEXAS
Miller Family Saga Series 2
The New Cowboy at Miller Ranch Prologue

Humbling Her Cowboy

In Debt to the Cowboy

The Cowboy Falls for the Veterinarian

Almost Fired by the Cowboy

Faking a Date with Her Cowboy Boss

Miller Brothers of Texas Complete Collection

BRIDES OF MILLER RANCH, N.M.

Miller Family Saga Series 3

Cowgirl Fallin' for the Single Dad

Cowgirl Fallin' for the Ranch Hand

Cowgirl Fallin' for the Neighbor

Cowgirl Fallin' for the Miller Brother

Cowgirl Fallin' for Her Best Friend's Brother

Cowboy Fallin' in Love Again

Brides of Miller Ranch Complete Collection

Miller Family Wrap-up Story

(An update on all your favorite characters!)

~

Copper Creek Romances

BAKER BROTHERS OF COPPER CREEK

Copper Creek Romances Series 1

Cowboys & Protective Ways

Cowboys & Crushes

Cowboys & Christmas Kisses

Cowboys & Broken Hearts

Cowboys & Second Chances

Cowboys & Wedding Woes

Cowboys' Mom Finds Love

Baker Brothers of Copper Creek Complete Collection

CALLAHANS OF COPPER CREEK

Copper Creek Romances Series 2

Making a Cowgirl

Marrying a Cowgirl

Christmas with a Cowgirl

Trusting a Cowgirl

Dating a Cowgirl

Catching a Cowgirl

Loving a Cowgirl

Marrying a Cowboy

Callahans of Copper Creek Complete Collection

KEAGANS OF COPPER CREEK

Copper Creek Romances Series 3

Some Cowboys are Off-Limits

Some Cowgirls Love Single Dads

Some Cowboys are Infuriating

Some Cowboys Don't Like City Girls

Some Cowboys Heal Broken Hearts

Some Cowgirls are Worth Protecting

Some Cowboys are Just Friends (Coming August 2024)

Though I try to keep this list updated in each book, you may also visit my website nataliedeanauthor.com for the most up to date information on my book list.

CONTENTS

1

Silas

Hooves pounded against the earth in a thunderous rush, the ground flying below at a break-neck speed. It was exhilarating, the morning sun shining on his back, the crisp air in his lungs, sharp with the lingering cold of winter but rich with the possibility of the new life of spring.

Silas and his mount, Amaranth, cut across the riding trail with confidence, his twin brother right behind him. He could practically feel Sterling breathing down his back, close to catching up with him, but not quite close enough.

Then it happened. With one more press of his heel, Amaranth was rushing forward in one last lunge, taking him across their impromptu line of finish-barrels. It took him a bit to kill his momentum, but when he did, he saw his twin giving him a rueful look from his own mount, Obelisk.

"I would maybe feel slighted, but I know you've been practicing your riding more than me."

Silas sent his brother a grin. "That's not exactly hard to do. When was the last time you walked to any of our barns? Or hung out with the horses?"

"Yeah, yeah, go ahead and lecture me. What's with all the outdoor time you've been racking up lately? I feel like I hardly ever see you or Solomon anymore."

"We're around," he answered with a shrug. "Besides, we had a particularly hard winter. Now that spring is here, figured it'd be good to get out and enjoy things, ya know?"

Sterling let out an amused huff. "That's one way to put it. I thought Dad was going to have an outright apoplexy when Samuel called us to say that he was getting engaged to some farmhand. I don't think I've ever heard 'prenup' so many times in a single screaming-fit."

Silas returned his wan smile. "Yeah, that was definitely an interesting day."

It wouldn't have been that bad if that was the only surprise event that happened. And as the two slowly trotted to the horse barn and went through grooming their mounts, Silas couldn't help but mentally go through everything else that had happened.

For one, Solomon and the strange city girl that he was with seemed to be getting pretty serious. He rarely ever talked about it, and Silas wasn't sure that Dad even knew about it, but it was definitely affecting things.

It wasn't anything too obvious, Silas supposed, but he noticed a pattern after Solomon started spending way more time in his office and started going to the city a couple of times a week. He and Dad fought more than Silas could ever remember in his entire life, the tension in the house rising with each passing feud. He wished that the two of them could find an accord, but it seemed that Solomon wasn't willing to be Pa's errand boy anymore. And as Solomon was being groomed to take over as head of the business, he had new ideas of how things should be run that their dad adamantly disagreed with.

As if his dad had heard his thoughts, Silas' phone rang as he went to get a treat for Amaranth. He was half-tempted not to answer his phone, surprising himself by the very thought. He never ignored his dad's calls.

Huh.

Answering, he wasn't surprised to hear his dad's sour tone on the other end. Dad was always mad about something lately. Mom said it was the election stress mounting, but Silas wasn't entirely enthused about the man Dad was trying to get into the position of power. Not that he would ever say that out loud, of course.

Dad spoke with his usual commanding voice. "I need you to go into the city, to that one property we put in a proposal for and check if it's worth doing a follow-up on."

"Oh?" Silas tried to ask nonchalantly. It was no secret that he'd always had a knack for telling if a new land acquisition was going to be a good investment or not. But he thought that his family was currently more into streamlining the processes that they already had than expanding.

"Yes. A new opportunity has opened up, and we might have a chance to seize this at half cost. But I want to make sure that it's going to be worth it. You know how you have a nose for sniffing out hang-ups."

"Alright, Dad. When do you want me to head out?"

"Now."

"Now?"

"Yes, now. That's what I pay you for, right?"

Silas held his tongue. He hated it when his dad brought up his salary because it wasn't like he could argue with that. Still, it would be nice to be *asked* to drop everything and go to the city rather than being ordered like some little Boy Scout.

"Alright, Pa. Email me the address and whatever specs we already have. I'll look around and do some digging."

"That's my boy."

The call ended as abruptly as it started, Sterling giving him a stern look.

"See, I told you being talented would only end up in trouble," Sterling said.

"Don't I know it. I'll see you later."

"Alright. But I won't stay up for you."

"You never do."

They shared a dry laugh. For being twins, they certainly had plenty of differences. While Silas liked to roll out of bed around nine and start his day, Sterling always had problems sleeping through the night. It had caused plenty of issues when they were kids, but it had leveled out since they had separate rooms—albeit in the same wing.

Lately, the younger twin had taken to sleeping from ten to midnight, then somewhere around four a.m. to six a.m., then again from one o'clock to whenever the heck he woke up in the afternoon. It probably wasn't the greatest for him, but it was what seemed to work. Silas got the feeling that sometimes his brother envied how the rest of his siblings could sleep whenever they wanted to, but Sterling never verbalized as much.

Besides, it wasn't like anything could be done about it. He'd done enough sleep studies for them to know that he was perfectly healthy, and he didn't want to risk addiction to sleep aids, so it was what it was. Besides, Silas had enough on his plate without having to think about his little brother's sleeping habits.

After taking care of his horse, he hopped in a golf cart and headed back toward the house. He used to drive to the barn, but Solomon was on a kick about the environment and reducing their waste where they could, and Mom had been suspiciously excited to suggest electric-powered golf cart-like things.

Although, it had been pretty darn adorable when her lilac golf cart was delivered, with flowers painted onto its covering and protective, clear rain curtains that could be rolled down the sides whenever the weather eventually kicked in. She'd fluttered around like a kid on Christmas, even though she could have bought it whenever she wanted, considering that their family was solidly in the billions in net worth.

That pleasant memory lasted through getting his car and heading into the city. He would have liked to read through the entire file, but he didn't multitask while he drove. That's what Sterling was for.

Except he and his twin rarely did any jobs together anymore. Mostly because they traded off dealing with Pa's special events or business meetings and parties. It wasn't like most people could tell them apart anyway.

Which was ridiculous, because Silas didn't think that they looked *that* similar.

Sure, they shared the same face and eyes, but Silas kept his hair cut shorter in the classic, Americana style while Sterling favored a slightly curly almost-bouffant look. There was also the matter of the scar—

Silas shook his head. He didn't need to think about that at the moment. He just needed to drive.

And so, he did. Arriving somewhere around ten thirtyish. It

was the perfect time, really. Early enough to miss any lunch rushes but late enough that many of the local workers would be at wherever they were employed. Silas found his job was the easiest when he could snoop without gaining much attention.

It took about an hour and twenty minutes to get to the exit he wanted, all the way on the other side of the city, and he pulled into a clearly abandoned shopping center that the rest of the residents were using for parking. A quick scan of all the cars in the area told him that not a single one of them was new, and most were patched up in some sort of rough way. Alright, that meant the residents were most likely in the lower class, but not so low that they couldn't afford a vehicle—even if a majority of them were beaters.

He was almost tempted to get out of the car and hurry through the process so that he could get home, but he decided he didn't want to rush it and have to come back. Unlike Solomon, he had no desire for repeated trips to the city.

So instead he sat back and read the file. There were at least three other competitors who were interested in the properties and had been putting out feelers too. Part of the reason Dad was probably interested in the entire block was just to spite them as much as it would be a great spot for another warehouse.

Because it would be a great place for a warehouse, that was for sure. It was practically immediately off the highway, so easy access for deliveries. It was on a sketchier side of the city, so the price of gobbling it up wouldn't be that extreme. Also, if they got their warehouse there so that they could supply more grocers on the other side of the city, it would raise the property value of the entire effort and provide a healthy return on their investment if they ever sold the place. Especially since there was a luxury apartment building being constructed not that far away.

It took him a good half hour to look over everything he wanted to, check out all the info and specs he could find online. But eventually he locked the file in his glove compartment and headed out.

His brothers always thought he was crazy for bringing his expensive car to the rougher parts of town, but he wasn't particularly attached, and it was insured. It wasn't like his brother's car, which was some souped-up, sporty thing that cost a real mint.

He walked the front of the block, and then the back, then repeated the process on the other side. He took his time, making sure to jot down which were businesses and which were residences. For the first time in a while, almost all of the shops had apartments directly above them, where he guessed the owners lived. Interesting, and the sign of a close community.

But there were other parts that showed it as being less close. There were a lot of young folks, ranging from grade school to their early twenties, some playing, some milling about, some very clearly busy on errands, some working and some loitering around. If there was one thing Silas had learned from his several years of helping his dad, it was that when kids had to act like adults, their homelife was less than ideal.

The power lines in the neighborhood were old, and pairs of shoes hung over a couple. He spotted a pothole, a few shuttered windows, a few with bars over them. But he also spotted a community grocery with people laughing and shopping. He saw older people sitting on porches. There was an undercurrent of community, but it was a weaker one.

Interesting.

It took him longer than he thought it would to finish up, especially since he wanted to get home and see if Mom needed help in her garden, but after two full hours and several dozen instances of some serious side-eye, he was heading back to his car.

He almost expected trouble: a broken window or someone showing up and demanding to know why he was poking around the neighborhood. But instead there was no one there, no damage to his car, and he was able to slide in without incident.

Alright, Silas could do with some more good luck like that. He put in one of his favorite CDs and started to pull out.

Only to have his car sputter out and his steering wheel to freeze like a rock.

He had jinxed it... hadn't he...

Biting his tongue, Silas refrained from letting out a long list of curses. He was sure his dad would have some sort of lecture about car maintenance or something of the sort, but he didn't want to call someone to tow him all the way back to the manor.

Getting out of his car, Silas looked around, his hands on his hips. In a strange twist of luck again, he saw that there was a mechanic shop right down the road. Huh, the day really was an emotional rollercoaster, wasn't it?

Shrugging his shoulders, he headed back down the street again.

2

———————

Silas

The mechanic shop wasn't bad, as far as mechanic shops went. The building had a sort of reception office that was connected to the garage. Of course, the front lot was filled with cars that looked like they could use some help, and Silas was sure the back was cluttered with parts and scraps. He had noticed it vaguely when he'd been walking along but hadn't paid much attention. Mechanic shops usually did good business in low-income areas, with everyone needing their car to survive but always owning vehicles on the verge of death. It was a cruel cycle, but if they saved up, they would be able to get less of a junker. Besides, there was public transportation and biking.

He shook his head, catching his derailed train of thought. Walking up to the cluttered front desk, he stood there for a moment. There was a young man in a jumpsuit there, the standard blue one you might expect on someone who worked in a garage. He couldn't have been much older than eighteen, with short locks framing his round face and thick glasses over his umber eyes. He didn't seem too busy, and yet a couple minutes passed by, then a couple more.

Silas stood there quietly, shifting slightly from foot to foot. He didn't want to interrupt in case the young man was filling out an invoice or trying to concentrate on something important, but he couldn't help but feel like maybe he was being ignored.

Silas wasn't used to being ignored.

He waited another two minutes before gently clearing his throat. The young man still hesitated for a moment then finally looked up, rubbing his nose with the back of his hand that resulted in a smear of grit across his dark skin. Silas decided not to say anything about that. Maybe it was petty, but who was to say?

"You need directions to the highway, sir?" Well, at least he was polite.

"No, actually. My car just stalled out. I was hoping to get a tow and see if you guys had time to take a look at it?"

The young man scratched his nose again, resulting in another smear. Silas still didn't say anything. "Umm... hold on a minute. Let me go check with the mechanics. You can have a seat over there." He pointed to a line of three folding chairs pressed up against the far wall.

"Alright. I'll do that, then."

It wasn't quite the brush off, but it wasn't exactly a warm customer service welcome either. Silas couldn't tell if he was too used to being kissed up to and pampered or if he had somehow annoyed the receptionist even as he walked in. But he started to think it was the latter more than the former when it took another twenty minutes for the young man to return.

"Yeah, Dante says that he can head out to tow your car. You're gonna ride along, right?"

"Uh, sure. Right." Not exactly what he had been expecting, but maybe that was how things were done in this neighborhood. He certainly wasn't going to object.

But... as it just so happened, he kind of wished he had. By the time one of the workers grabbed a rusted, beaten old tow truck and got it to Silas' car, that feeling of being unwanted had grown much more. When they eventually made it back to the mechanic's shop, Silas was about ready to climb out of his own skin.

He was charming. Normally people liked him. He couldn't figure out what he had said or done to make a whole shop take offense to him. He wasn't wearing anything political, even religious really. He had an old cross on a necklace that was from his great-grandmother, but it was small and hidden under both his shirt and his undershirt. Besides, judging by the Lord's prayer that was framed behind the desk, the business wasn't going to take offense to Christian iconography.

His family didn't have any bad blood in the area either. And he hadn't introduced himself, so no one even knew that he was a Miller. And even if they did know he was a Miller, they didn't know he was one of *the* Millers.

He didn't climb out of his own skin, however, and instead climbed out of the tow truck. Silas wished he was back on the ranch. His hands were itching to do something productive, to get on his horse or go check on the cows. Maybe do some fishing at the large pond Dad had built when Silas was barely old enough to remember. The family used to have picnics there when the summer sun was hot and the water was cool, but that had stopped too.

Why had that happened? Why had they all... drifted apart? Silas couldn't quite remember, and the details weren't going to come back to him while he was standing in the middle of a strange mechanic's yard. He was beginning to wish that he had called his brother and one of their on-call guys, but he was already committed to his decision.

There was a flurry of activity and noise that Silas stayed out of the way for, but then, when it settled, he saw two mechanics looking over his car, which already had been placed onto a lift.

Except one of the mechanics wasn't anything at all like he had expected.

She was fairly tall and with a figure that was evident even through her mechanic's jumpsuit. She was a redhead, almost flamingly so, but there was a shock of white hair at one of her temples. It was a strange fashion choice, one that Silas hadn't seen before. The kind that Mom would call ostentatious. He just thought it made her stand out compared to the blues and grease stains and metal of the mechanic shop. She was young, as well. She looked even younger than Silas, and yet the body language of everyone seemed like they were deferring to her.

Well, if there was anyone who probably had an idea of what was going on, it was her. Striding across the lawn, he went into the garage, stopping far enough back that he hoped he would be out of the way.

"Hey, how are you? How's the—"

"You shouldn't be here," she said brusquely, not even looking up. "Insurance hazard. Please wait in the reception area."

"I just wanted to ask—"

"I'm still in the process of examining your car. I'll need time. Please be patient and go wait. In the reception area."

Silas was good with people, he really was, so it grated against his nerves that suddenly everyone and their mom seemed thoroughly irritated with him.

"I'm sorry, did I do something wrong?" he said, trying to sound more amused than perturbed. "Seems like everybody's giving me the cold shoulder around here."

The young woman turned to him, and he was struck again by how young she looked. She couldn't be past her mid-twenties. She had a button nose, her eyes angled in a slightly cat-like way. She was quite pale, with cherubic cheeks that made her seem like she'd be the cheerful sort.

Except the look she was giving him wasn't anywhere near cheerful.

"I don't know, maybe because we all know why you're here."

"Why I'm here?"

She furrowed her brows. "Don't play dumb. You're another rich businessman here to push us all out of our homes and snatch up our businesses to make room for more of your rich friends to buy things away from us rabble."

Silas blinked at her a moment, surprised by her description. The way she said it made him and his family sound like bad guys. They were looking to invigorate the local economy and give everyone they purchased land from a tidy little boost.

"We're not—"

She held up her hand, already turning back to his vehicle. "You're here to have your car fixed, so let me fix your car so you can go back and tell them everything you've dug up about us."

The thing was, what she was saying would have come out as scathing from anyone else. But from her, it was more...

matter of fact. Like there wasn't even a point in arguing because it just was the way it was. Plus, Silas was still shocked by the fact that she seemed to know that he was there for acquisition purposes and even more shocked at the picture she'd painted about him.

Also... *another* rich businessman? Had his competitors already been skulking around?

"Alright. I'll, uh, I'll be in the reception area then."

Silas turned and walked quickly away. He felt like he needed to defend himself, but also that it would be rude to do so. Plus, he didn't want to tick off the people who were supposed to work on his car any more than they already were. And even though they were... less than pleasant, they were helping him. The tow had been smooth—although awkward —and the worker had done his best not to damage or scratch anything. They unloaded his car and got it onto the lift carefully as well.

Silas wasn't used to being so off-center, but that was exactly how he felt as he wondered if he should call his brother or not. And the whole debate turned out to be pointless because about ten minutes later, the redhead was walking into the reception area.

"So, good news, your car has a real easy fix. Probably only an hour of work."

Silas stepped forward, still feeling uncertain. "Your tone implies there's bad news."

She nodded. "Yeah, we need to order the part. You've got a sporty ride out there, so it's not really something we keep around. You're looking at a couple of days. If you have a guy or a shop that you think would fix it faster, we can arrange for a tow of your car there, on the house."

Silas blinked at her again. He hadn't been expecting that.

"You'd do that even though I would be taking my business elsewhere?"

"Of course. It's not your fault that we don't carry the part, and here at Andre's, we're more interested in making sure everyone can get home safe."

"That's... uh, that's a good motto."

There was a strange expression on her face as she regarded him. "Yeah. It is."

Silas wasn't quite sure why he said what he did, but then his mouth was opening, and he was giving her an amiable smile. "No, I don't have a guy. If it takes a couple of days, it takes a couple of days."

It was her turn to look surprised, although she covered it quickly. For some reason, that amused him a touch more than it should have.

"Alright then. You have a way home?"

"I'll call my brother to pick me up. In the meantime, you have a recommendation for someplace I can grab some food?"

Her stare was bordering on unnerving as she evaluated, and Silas couldn't help but wonder what exactly she was looking for. Whatever it was, she seemed to find her answer because she was talking again.

"Mar-Ray's is down the street. Got the best Jamaican and soul food. It's owned by this great couple who've been around for ages."

Silas couldn't help but feel like she had a very pointed reason for her recommendation, but good food was good food. "Thanks. I'll keep that in mind."

3

Theodora

*T*eddy was *starving.* It had been a long day, especially with the arrival of that blatantly obvious business shark that dropped in toward the end of the day. At first she had almost thought that his supposed broken-down car was some sort of con, some way to get more information from them, but after examining it, she realized that no, he just happened to have some bad luck and his fancy car had actually broken down.

At least he got out of their hair quickly, and she'd closed up the shop after that and headed upstairs with Roman and a couple others. And they all definitely scrambled, because it was Andre's night to cook and everyone knew that he made the best meals out of any of them. It was the main reason that she hadn't just run across the street to Salina's or Mar-Ray's. She didn't want to fill her belly when her father's quality cooking was on the table.

Now, if it was *Roman*, his son, that would be an entirely different matter. Teddy loved her brother, but the man was not gifted in the kitchen. Not like his pop.

Warm, happy smells greeted her as soon as she opened the door leading into their apartment right above the shop. It wasn't the biggest place, but it was a three-bedroom and that was all the space they needed. Even though it was crowded around dinner time with all their visitors that tended to drop by.

"Hey there," Andre said from the kitchen, turning down a couple of the burners. "Dinner's almost done. You want to set the table?"

"Roman can do that," Teddy said, pulling her bandana off and reaching for her brush she always kept by the door. She had her mother's hair in more than one respect, and her wild, frizzy curls always ended up even wilder after a full day in her dad's shop.

"Excuse me, you're the youngest. Since when do you order me around?" Roman said.

"Don't act like that's new boy," Andre called from the kitchen with a laugh. "She's been bossing you around since the day you met and ain't nothing changed."

Roman grumbled under his breath in that good-natured way only a beleaguered older sibling could. He was a good egg, her brother. All strapping muscles and basically the spitting image of their father, his hair in artfully arranged locks. Teddy was pretty sure he could have been a male model if he wanted, but he'd chosen to stick around the shop, just like her.

She couldn't blame him. The world was a cold place and Andre's hearth was always so warm. He was the kindest man that she had ever known, and she'd met quite a few people in her twenty-four years on earth.

"Hey, Boss. That's a nice apron you have there." That was Jameel, one of the newer hires.

"You're darn right it is," Andre said with a grin that made him look younger despite his short, salt and pepper hair. "Teddy made it for me when she was thirteen in home-ec class."

The worker's eyes flicked to Teddy, and she just shrugged. She wasn't exactly known as the most feminine person or for being interested in the creative arts, but that was how she liked to keep it. She was a relatively private person, and the less other people outside of her circle knew her, the better. At least in her opinion.

"Alright, table's set," Roman said, sticking his head in from the small kitchen. "We got milk, water and OJ."

They all said what they wanted and headed to the kitchen. While Teddy liked her privacy, she didn't mind that her dad always had an open kitchen policy. The world was a pretty scary, cruel place, and she hated the thought of anyone being hungry. Besides, as her mother had always said, food was better shared, and there were plenty of hungry people in the community to share with.

"Let's say grace," Andre said once everyone was seated, and they joined hands. It was nice, the tradition. A comfort that had started when she'd been ten and had continued for four-teen years. She wasn't very good at praying out loud herself, but her dad certainly had a knack for it. Teddy thought that he should teach more lessons at the church—the only day of the week the shop was closed—but Andre would always say he wasn't one for public speaking.

"Amen," they all said together, and then Teddy was digging in with gusto.

It was *good*. Because it was always good. The warm food hit her belly in just the right way, and she inhaled it perhaps faster than she should have. If the other two workers thought anything about her ravenous chow-down, they didn't say anything, but that might have been because their mouths were full too.

"Hey, slow down there, Teddy. The food will still be there in a couple minutes," her dad said.

"Not if I have anything to say about it," Roman said and laughed, reaching his fork over and spearing one of the bites of pork chop that she had cut.

"Don't you dare!" Teddy objected, covering her mouth with one hand and snatching at the piece of meat with her fingers. Thus started a quick grab-battle with her brother that lasted approximately a half minute before Andre cleared his throat.

"Sorry," the siblings said, but Teddy still stuck her tongue out at her brother.

"Huh, I've never seen you like this," Jameel said, not unkindly, an amused expression on his face.

"Don't let her fool you," Hassan said, chuckling lightly. "She just likes to pretend to be all hard edges in the shop. Make us think she's one of those mean ones."

"Can you blame me?" Teddy asked with a shrug. "You've seen how some customers treat me."

Jameel rolled his eyes. "You ain't kidding. You think they'd be havin' a straight-up heart attack just because a lady touched their car. It's the twenty-first century. My mom was the one who taught me how to change my oil."

Teddy smiled at that. It was always a gamble with new folks, but she was glad that Jameel seemed to be one of the good ones. Her dad had a real knack for choosing good employees. The only reason he'd needed a replacement was because Hyacinth, the other female mechanic, had gotten pregnant and decided to become a stay-at-home mom after her hubby got a promotion at his government job. Hyacinth had been whip-sharp and took absolutely no crap. Teddy missed her.

"How is your mother, Jameel? I haven't seen her in church lately," Andre said.

"Still on that cruise. Why you asking?" Jameel smirked, and it was such an impish expression that Teddy almost wanted to pinch his cheek. "She's single, you know."

That had Roman coughing on his water and even Teddy found herself snorting in surprise.

"Why, young man, you act like you're trying to set me up," Andre said.

"And what if I was? You're a good man, Boss. I wouldn't mind seein' my ma taken care of by a good man."

Andre shifted uncomfortably. "Uh, well, I—"

His stilted response was cut off as a buzzer sounded, a small light flickering in the corner of their kitchen.

"Oh, what's that?" Hassan asked, craning his neck behind him.

"Another one of Teddy's strays," Roman said, rolling his eyes.

She was well aware that he disagreed with some of the things she did, but he never did much besides grumble about it.

"I got it," Teddy said, standing up quickly. "You talk more about this dating business. I'm sure Pops would *love* to hear more about your ma."

Okay, maybe that wasn't the *nicest* thing to do, but sometimes Andre needed a shove. And he definitely needed one when it came to his romantic life. As far as she knew, he'd been single well before she met him, never having quite gotten over his falling-out with Roman's mother and the ensuing custody battle. He'd dated a couple women very casually, but it never even got far enough for him to ever bring one of the nice ladies home.

Which didn't make sense to Teddy. Her dad was the most loving, caring, forgiving and warm person in the world. It was probably fair to call her a Daddy's Girl, but how could she not be, considering how amazing he was? Growing up, she had plenty of friends who had parents who were borderline abusive or actually so. Considering how rocky her life had started, she really had been blessed with Andre.

She made it downstairs to the door all the way at the back of the garage. The corner tucked right against the alley, on a blind spot of the shop. The buzzer blared again, and she opened it to see Antonio, one of the young locals who had a real knack for getting into trouble.

"You look terrible," she said bluntly, standing to the side to allow him in. He was a tall, scrap of a teenager, all full of lean muscle and too many scars.

"Thanks, Mami. And you're just as pretty as ever."

"Yeah, yeah, Casanova. Let me get a good look at you in the light."

He followed her over to where she kept the first aid kit in the other corner of the shop, along with an eye washing station and sink. Flicking the switch, she gripped his chin gently and tilted it up to give it a good look.

He was busted up pretty badly, but it wasn't the worst he'd ever been, and it certainly wasn't the worst she'd ever seen.

With a sigh, she went about cleaning his cuts first then going about patching him up.

"Do I even want to know what you were up to this time, huh?" she asked, his blood a stark contrast on her pale skin. Geez, maybe she really did need to leave the shop once in a while. She was turning into a ghost. Maybe she was using a bit *too* much sunscreen when she was out in the garden.

"You never do, Mami. You know that."

"It's Teddy," she corrected for probably the hundredth time. "And aren't you tired of showing up here, battered in the middle of the night? If you made new friends, got involved with a better crowd, you wouldn't—"

"*God*, Teddy, can we not do this while I'm bleeding right now?"

"Don't take the Lord's name in vain. At least not here."

"You really think that God cares about someone like me?" the teenager scoffed.

Now that... that really stabbed at Teddy's heart. Sure, Antonio was rough about the edges, but people cared for him. *She* cared for him. "He cares about us especially."

"Yeah, well it don't feel like it most of the time. You know Malia's grandma died yesterday? Her insulin was so expensive that she stopped taking it so she wouldn't be a burden anymore."

Teddy's stomach sank as she continued to work. She hadn't heard that. Malia and her weren't close, but she remembered them praying for her family after her father was deported and her mother had to take on extra jobs. He'd overstayed his visa from Russia.

Antonio continued, "And those rich guys are sending more and more of their saps. Rumor is they're getting their fingers involved on the streets."

Teddy scoffed outright at that. "Please. Getting involved means they have to acknowledge us as people."

He smiled, but it was bitter, and the huff that left his lips was toned with pain. "I mean, you may have a point there."

Teddy thought back to the handsome, incredibly well-dressed man who showed up in the shop and it made her heart sink further. She didn't want to talk about any of that. It was erasing the warm safety and comfort that she always found when the day ended and it was dinnertime with her family.

"Sit still and let me see your knuckles. I bet they're busted again."

"Your powers of recognizing patterns continue to be the best, Mami."

"Teddy."

"Whatever you say."

He did settle, and Teddy absently heard her two coworkers eventually exit and both Andre and Roman settle down for the night. She finished up tending to Antonio, and when she was satisfied, she ruffled his unkempt hair.

"Come on, let's go get you fed."

He gave her a skeptical look. "That depends. Whose night was it?"

She ruffled his hair a bit harder. "You know that you've been over way too much when you know about our cooking schedule. And it was Andre, just so you know."

"Ah, your daddy? Yeah, gimme some of that." Antonio gave her a charming smile.

Teddy laughed and led Antonio up the stairs.

"Hey, why do you call him your dad but also by his first name?"

Teddy shrugged, opening up the door to the apartment. "I dunno really. I suppose it might be because, when I first met him, he was just Andre. He wasn't really my dad until three years later. I guess I kinda use them interchangeably."

"Huh. Sounds confusing. But it's cool he adopted you and all that."

Teddy sent him a shocked expression. "What? How did you know I'm adopted?"

For a singular moment, Antonio looked so surprised his face paled. But then the moment passed, and he gave her an unappreciative look. "You think you're funny, don't you?"

"What? You don't think a redheaded ghost could come from Andre? You never know what's in someone's genetic history."

"Yeah, yeah, you think you're *real* funny."

She did chuckle lightly. Andre clearly knew from the moment the buzzer sounded that she would end up feeding someone, and a plate was already sitting in the microwave. Heating it up for half a minute, she grabbed some juice and set a place for Antonio at the table.

"Thanks, Mami."

"You keep up with that and I'm gonna stop feeding you."

"Yeah, you say that, but I'll believe it when I see it, Mother Teresa."

Teddy rolled her eyes and went about getting herself a glass of water then washing some more dishes while Antonio forked his food down. It didn't seem possible, but he devoured it even quicker than she had, and soon he was staring regretfully down at his empty plate.

"I need to wash up and get to bed soon, but I'll pack you something to go. How does that sound?"

"You always treat me so well, Mami. When you gonna let me take you out and do something special for you?"

He sent her a look that almost for certain was supposed to

be a smolder, but it just made her laugh. "Call me if you suddenly age ten years in a day."

"Ten years? You're not that much older than me."

"I'm twenty-four and what are you… thirteen?"

Oooh, the glare that she earned from that was gold. "You know I turned seventeen last month. You baked me a cake."

"No, *Andre* baked you a cake. I frosted it because his hands hurt a lot. I'm sure there are plenty of girls your age you can take on a date if you ever stop getting the tar beaten out of your face."

"Aw, but I ain't interested in girls my age. I'm interested in—"

Teddy knew that Antonio was just being a heartbreaker teen, and if she was around his age, maybe she would have been affected. But instead she held out the doggie bag that she had made. "If you don't stop with that, you're gonna have to eat this off the alley outside."

"Ay, you know it's a sin to waste this good food like that, right?"

"Uh-huh, well don't make me waste it then. Behave yourself."

He held out his hands, and she pushed the container into it. Once he was done chugging his juice, she escorted him back down and gave him a hug before seeing him out the door. Despite all the slick game he tried to spit, he kept the hug exactly as it was supposed to be, an act of comfort between two people who cared for each other. Because she did care for him. She cared about so many in her community, even if she tended to seal herself away in the shop for days on end.

She stood at the door until he disappeared down the alleyway, hopefully back home and not into more trouble, then

headed back inside. She did make triple sure to lock everything up; then it was up the stairs and into the apartment.

Teddy didn't expect to see Andre standing there, looking
over the empty plate and cup. It was strange to see him up, as
usually once he settled into his room, he would pass out in
either his bed or his chair after reading a good book.

"Ya need something?" she asked, standing on tiptoe to give
him a peck on the cheek. But the look that he gave her made
her pause, and she tilted her head to the side.

"I know I may not be the most verbose man, but I wanted
you to know that I couldn't be prouder of the woman you've
become. And your mother would be too."

Oh.

That was... she hadn't been expecting that.

"Thanks, Dad."

"Of course, sweet pea. You have a good night now. I'll see
you in the morning. Love you."

As it always did, her heart swelled in her chest. With all the
terrible things that were happening in the world, she would
always have Andre and Roman. Her family. "Love you too."

4

———

Silas

"Did you want to stop for a soda?"

Silas paused for a moment, looking up from some of the power grid specs he was looking at to think about it. "I... you know what, no. I just want to get to my car. If I get a sugar craving, I'll pick up one on my way back home."

"Sounds like a plan."

"Thanks again for driving me. I appreciate it."

Solomon shrugged. "I was heading into the city to visit with Frenchie anyway. It's no skin off my back."

"Right. Your girl."

"Don't say it like that."

Silas affixed his second oldest brother with a plain look. "Like what?"

"I dunno. Just... like that."

"Alright then, I'll try not to say it 'like that,' whatever 'like that' is."

Solomon narrowed his eyes at him, but the look wasn't nearly that withering because he quickly had to return his gaze to the road. Besides, Solomon was pretty used to the ribbing, considering that was Silas' main method of showing affection. Which was slightly better than Sterling's outright teasing that could sometimes go too far. His brother was really doing him a solid by giving him a ride. Dad would have no doubt been confused and far too curious as to why Silas had chosen to let a run-down shop in the city take care of his car. Especially since he didn't really know himself.

Clearly, he hadn't made a bad choice because the car was ready a whole day earlier than they had quoted him. He just hoped they did good work. But when he thought about the woman he met there and the intense way she'd studied his car before telling him off, he couldn't help but feel like he had left his vehicle in good hands. And maybe he was naive for thinking that considering the way she had talked to him, but she struck him as the type of woman who was proud of her work.

He and Solomon drove along in relative quiet after that, leaving Silas to his thoughts. Which he had a lot of. His brother had been... different ever since he met the girl in the city. Silas didn't mind it, but it certainly was causing tension back home.

Funny, how his family was considered to have some of the most eligible bachelors in the state, but none of them really dated. Sure, all of them had tried once or twice, but it usually didn't end up working out. Between being busy, dodging gold diggers, and focusing on helping Dad build his empire, there wasn't room for much else. Sometimes Silas felt like they forgot what it was like to even be ranchers.

That thought unsettled him, not leaving even when his brother dropped him off at the shop and zoomed away, anxious to go see his mysterious city girl.

Shoving his phone into his pocket, he headed into the shop. The same young man was at the reception desk, but this time he didn't ignore Silas. No, instead he looked startled.

"What are you doing here?" It wasn't maliciously said, but it certainly gave him pause.

"I was called? For my car."

"You shouldn't have been called. Not yet." The young man looked frustrated. "Hold on. Lemme go talk to Jamal. He watched the desk for the first two hours of the day."

"Alright. You do that."

Why did it feel like stepping into the shop was the same as being transported to an entirely different world with unknown rules?

The young man came back out, looking even more stressed. "Apologies for having you come here too early. Your car was supposed to be finished, but there was an emergency with the Munch buses and both our owner and his daughter went to go take care of it. They have to sign off on your car before we can release it."

"Munch buses?" Silas asked dubiously, wondering if the young man was putting one over on him.

"The local charity meal delivery program. They have a couple trucks that take meals to the elderly, disabled or in need." The young man gave him a borderline scathing look. "I suppose you don't have any of those in your neck of the woods."

"No, we definitely don't."

"Right. Well your ride's a pretty nice one, and since we ordered the part from one of those expensive suppliers, only the owner or his children can sign off on it."

"You said the owner and his daughter are out. What about his other child?"

"This is his only day off. We can call him, but he might not answer right away."

Silas felt his irritation rising. He didn't want to be stranded again at the shop, but he felt like complaining about them helping a charity would be particularly selfish.

"I guess I'll... go for a walk. Call me when you get in touch with him? Or if there's an update?"

"Yeah, of course we'll do that. For what it's worth, sir, I am sorry. This shouldn't have happened."

The apology seemed genuine, and the young man was still wearing that stressed expression. Silas again got the impression that the shop prided itself on customer service, despite their frosty reception of him.

"Life happens. Just let me know."

"Of course, sir. Thank you for your understanding."

Sir. Interesting. That was certainly a change from the previous time. Silas gave him a nod then headed out, figuring that he could at least get some more investigation in while he was stuck in town.

He headed the opposite way he had started, meaning to scan buildings, look at foundations, examine traffic points that seemed important. Except the buildings kept drifting to the background as he noticed the people of the small community.

There was a particularly old woman sitting in a folding chair next to a cart full of flowers. Her skin was wrinkled and like tanned leather, wizened from her years. A few moments later, a young girl with large, large hair and long nails walked up to her, handing her a steaming cup of what looked like either tea or coffee and pressing a kiss to the older woman's cheek.

It was a sweet scene, and then the girl was walking off and the woman was waving at her. Silas couldn't tell if they were related—they certainly didn't look like each other at all—but he figured if he stared any longer it would be creepy, so he kept on walking.

He thought then maybe he could pull his thoughts together and concentrate, but he was distracted again. There was a couple dancing in front of a restaurant, someone playing drums as well. A small crowd was gathered around them, clapping and laughing and generally seeming to be having a great time. Silas couldn't tell if they all knew each other, or if it was impromptu, but that didn't seem to matter. They were all so in the moment. And it was only just before lunch. What did they have to dance about or celebrate?

He didn't know, and it didn't seem right to walk up to them and demand an explanation when he was already so clearly an outsider. So he kept on.

But the more he walked, the more he looked around, the more he felt like he saw the starts of stories. People unlike what he was used to. People who clearly had their own lives and journeys. It was so unlike anything he'd experienced before in his evaluations. It wasn't like him to be so... distracted.

And yet, that was exactly what he was.

In fact, he was so distracted that he hadn't even realized how much time had passed until his phone buzzed in his pocket. Pulled from his revelry, he realized that it was close to dusk. How long had he been walking?

He blinked at his phone and saw two missed calls from the

shop. Well that certainly wasn't great. Cursing to himself, he looked around and realized he had no idea where he was. He really had been in his head, hadn't he?

It was probably the whole situation throwing him off. Plugging the shop address into his GPS, he headed back. Quickly, with his head tucked down, he found a slither of apprehension up his spine. He was acutely aware that he was a well-dressed man in an unknown area who stuck out like a sore thumb. That was... that was risky. How many times had his dad told him about needing protection on the wrong side of town? There was a reason they all had kidnapping insurance and life insurance policies.

It would draw too much attention to run, so he just settled for walking very quickly, just on the cusp of maybe sprinting. He thought he vaguely recognized where he was going, but it wasn't until the GPS told him to walk down a brick alley that he killed his momentum.

There was *no* way he was going through an alley to get to his destination. Why was the GPS even leading him to what must be the back way? He would just keep walking around and find the front. It wouldn't be that hard.

He stepped back and looked to the left. But there wasn't a street there. No, the block kept on what looked like a good way. Well... there were worse puzzles he'd solved.

He headed that way, but as he reached the corner, the GPS kept yelling at him that he was adding time to reach his destination. Silas saw that the street was a diagonal that went nowhere in the direction he needed to go. Zooming in on the map, he realized that taking it *would* lead him to the front of the shop, but if he wanted to stick to the main streets, it was going to add a solid fifteen minutes to his walk.

Normally that was small beans. He'd been walking for

hours, after all. But it was growing increasingly darker by the second and his stomach was twisting harshly. Silas just wanted to get to familiar territory as soon as possible.

It would be a bad decision. He shouldn't go down that alley.

But it was so close, only five minutes if he went that way. That was it. What could happen in five minutes?

With one last look at the diagonal row of run-down buildings, he turned and headed toward the alley.

His shoulders were up by his ears as he walked along, and he swore every sound of the city had him jumping. He felt like there should have been more people around, and he also felt like he *heard* them, but when he looked around, he didn't see anyone. Where were the food delivery folks, the miscreants? The ragamuffins? It was ominously vacant.

Finally, the back of the mechanic's shop loomed at the point where two alleys met. A kind of odd layout, but they were in the older, run-down part of the city that had been made long before the founders knew it would one day be a sprawling metropolis in the desert.

Well, *kinda* desert.

He hadn't noticed before, but there was a tall fence cutting about half of the backyard from view, the other half containing the two large shutter doors. They certainly had a large plot for being in the city, even if it was the older part. Maybe there had been another building there, long ago? Obviously, it hadn't been a mechanic's shop forever considering when the area started to grow and when cars were invented.

The sight of the building flooded him with relief, and then he did start jogging forward. He was pretty sure he could cut up the driveway and then be around to the front. Hopefully there was still someone in the shop. It wasn't *that* late.

...was it?

He supposed he would find out.

He was almost there, a building away or so, when the sound of a small motor filled the alley and a group of five or so young men were coming toward him too fast to be on regular bikes but too slow to be on motorcycles.

That... that couldn't be good.

"You lost, man?" one of them said. He looked like the kind one might expect to run into in an alley on the wrong side of town.

"Nope, just heading to the mechanic shop. They have my car."

"Ay, he's that man who's been walking around. Casing the place," another said. Not too much different from the first.

"We got something you want, huh?"

Silas straightened and looked around. They outnumbered him; they probably had weapons. While his fists were curling at his sides, he knew he wouldn't stand a chance against them. Maybe Sal would, *maybe*, but not Silas.

"No, I'm just researching."

"Oh, researching? What, like this is a zoo?"

"No, not like that."

"Well, if you're at the zoo, you have to pay to get in, right? Did you pay your admission, rich boy?"

"He looks like a cowboy," one of them said and laughed. "Is there such a thing as a rich cowboy?"

Silas declined from stating his family's net worth. That seemed like the worst idea considering the situation.

"If you want admission, I'm glad to give you that. I have that in my wallet, which I'm going to grab from my pocket right now. Alright?" He carefully reached for it, opening up the leather to slip his ID from it before tossing it between him and the five. So much for thinking that the city was far too empty. "Take whatever you want."

"Yeah, I bet you're real used to doing that, aren't ya?" the one that seemed to be the leader asked, finally getting off his ride. Silas finally saw that it was a regular bike that had a motor attached to it in a way he didn't understand. Huh, that was wild. "Just coming in and taking whatever you want from people like us. They got a word for that, you know? Remix was just telling us about it. Weren't you, Remix?"

One of the smallest of the five, a skinny whip of a young man with close-shaved hair and a face so bony he was almost a skeleton. If he wasn't threatening Silas, he would have been tempted to feed the young man a burger. "G-g-g-gentri-fication."

"That's right. Gentrification." The leader grinned and took another step, picking up the wallet. "Are you surprised we know that word? You lot think we're so stupid, don't you? Just a bunch of punks who don't know no better than to be failures."

Oh boy, there was a whole lot to unpack there. "I don't think that."

"Sure, you don't," he said, taking the cash out of Silas' wallet then throwing the rest behind him. "You're just here to evaluate the place and push us to prosperity like some sort of... of... Remix, what was that trope thing you were talking about?"

"W-w-white sav-vior."

Oh. They called the kid Remix because he had a stutter. Wasn't *that* something?

The leader snapped his fingers. "Yes, that's it. A white savior to come save all us dumb ghetto folk who just *love* being poor."

There was that bite again. Was that how people saw him and his family? Silas didn't get it. They weren't trying to hurt anybody. In fact, his family's payoffs would definitely change some of their lives. And those that stayed on the edges of the development—if it was successful—would have a huge influx of business. It could be good for everyone.

So why was this group of wannabe gang members looking at him like *he* was the villain?

"Well, you can go back to whatever mansion you came from and tell your big ol' boss that you can't buy us off. Tell him you're not welcome here."

"I'll make sure your concerns are communicated."

Silas was puzzled. He would be lying if he said he wasn't nervous. But he wasn't going to kowtow to them either. He just wanted to de-escalate the situation and get home. If that meant being diplomatic... well, he had experience with that. Managing his dad's increasing temper tantrums was experience enough, along with navigating the rest of the politics needed to grow their family business as much as they had.

"I dunno," another said, lips pulling back from his teeth in a snarl. "How do we know he's gonna say it exactly how we want him to?"

"You know, that's a fair point," the leader said. Suddenly there was a knife in his hand, and Silas knew the situation wasn't de-escalating at all. "I guess we'll send the message ourselves then."

Silas broadened his stance and raised his hands, bending his knees slightly. If it was going to be a fight, he was going to go down swinging. He wasn't helpless; he knew that any fight with a knife usually ended in terrible injuries.

"Oh, he's keyed up for a fight, is he? Look at him, some sort of kung-fu cowboy. Well then giddy—"

His taunt was cut off by a jarring boom that filled the entire alley. It jolted all of them, and Silas looked past the young men to see none other than the woman from the mechanic shop.

Even in the dark, she was striking. Pale skin and bright hair, grease on her coveralls. She was standing next to one of the garage doors, a baseball bat in her hands. So that was how she'd made the boom.

"What the hell do you lot think you're doing? You know you're not welcome near this property."

They rounded on her and Silas was sure he was about to see a *real* fight go down, but Teddy seemed unbothered. She shifted, a hip out, and swinging the baseball bat behind her to rest on her shoulders. It was like something out of a movie, not possible, and yet that was exactly what Silas was seeing.

"What, your black daddy owns this alley too?"

"No," Teddy said, taking a step forward and if that wasn't a power move, Silas didn't know what was.

She wasn't the tallest woman, wasn't the most jacked he had ever seen, wasn't even the fattest, but she commanded the space like she was four times her size. The tension ramped up that much higher, to an impossible level, and Silas swore he saw the gangbangers wilt slightly.

"No, but that won't stop me from beating the ever-loving crap out of y'all."

The leader walked toward her a short way but stayed out of range of her bat. "Just 'cause you messed up a few faces you think you can take on all of us?"

"Nah," she said, clearing her throat and spitting just in front of the young man's shoes. "I know I can't. But I also know that I can take out at least three of you before you bring me down." She closed one eye and aimed her baseball bat out like a gun, sweeping over them all. "Wanna take bets on which one of you's it'd be?"

Incredible. It was so different from the icy, measured tone she'd taken with him before. She was all heat and bravado, about twenty feet tall and sure of herself as a hurricane. It was baffling. It was awe-inspiring. It was confusing.

It was... *hot.*

There was silence for a long moment, the tension spiraling ever upward until finally, it snapped.

"Whatever," the leader said, clicking his tongue. "Y'aint worth the sweat. Come on, let's go get some food."

And just like that, the group got back on their bikes and headed out, exchanging poisonous looks with the woman. She seemed to be completely unaffected, watching them with a bored expression before looking to Silas.

"Your car is ready," she said flatly, lowering the baseball bat and crossing to a smaller door.

Silas stared after her, feeling a bit like he was caught in mood-whiplash.

...who *was* this woman?

5

Theodora

*T*eddy was irritated.

Actually, that was putting it lightly. It'd been such a stressful, fraught day from start to finish, the last thing she had wanted was to come out of her garden to see five lowlifes on her father's property.

The long day had all started when they'd gotten a call from the local charity they worked with pretty often. They'd only been told about one car that needed some help to get on the road, but when they'd shown up, they'd found out that both of the vans the charity used were in need of repair.

So that was less than stellar and took both her and Andre way longer than it should have. But then after that, there had been some peripheral cars used for smaller errands that they'd worked on, and before either of them knew it, the day was practically gone.

So coming home and going through her nightly routine had been a huge relief. Relief that quickly dried up when she heard somewhat familiar voices in the alley. She'd grabbed the bat she kept above the mechanic shop door then headed out, unsurprised to see a group of young men that she had run into before.

It wasn't all of the mini-gang, which numbered maybe about fifteen young men in total—all in their late teens and early twenties. To say they didn't get along with the shop was putting it mildly, but they had a loose sort of stalemate because all of their families and younger siblings loved either her, her father or the shop. If Teddy ran to their *abuelas* or moms and tattled, the sky would rain down on them.

But that unspoken truce didn't cover the rich man whose car was in her shop, and that was exactly who they had cornered.

What was he even doing in the alley? Didn't he have a lick of sense?

"Thank you for that," he said, approaching her as she finished unlocking the door to the inside.

"Bad for business if some rich guy gets killed right outside of our shop."

"Uh... thanks for the concern."

She scoffed and headed inside. She was tired and cranky, and she was also irritated with the rich man for coming in and trying to poach her neighborhood. The community around her was hard built, with families and stories going back for generations. They opened their hearts and homes to her after everything had happened with her mother. Welcomed her with open arms even though she was pale and prickly and... well, *her*.

"Anyway, I apologize for the scheduling error. We had some

emergencies come up suddenly and our fill-in for the receptionist didn't get the memo in time. He was trying to be helpful. As an apology, we'd like to offer you ten percent off."

He blinked at her like he was surprised. That irritated her too. He was always looking at her like she had grown another head. She knew that she wasn't what people pictured when they thought of a mechanic, but that didn't mean he needed to *stare* at her.

"Oh no, that's fine. You were helping out a charity. It'd be pretty terrible of me to complain about that, or demand compensation."

That wasn't what she expected. She had to admit, she had a pretty unimpressed view of the wealthy for the most part. "Huh."

"You sound surprised."

He was smirking in a charming way, but instead of soothing her, it just made her feel on the defensive. He was just so... so... *pretty*. No. That wasn't quite the right word. *Handsome.* She was usually too busy to care about such things. The last time she'd had a crush or really noticed a man was in high school, with Marquis White. He'd been in her shop class, and she'd always gotten so tongue-tied around him, even when they'd finally gone on a date.

But the man in front of her, although he was the complete opposite of Marquis, was undeniably attractive.

Add that to the list of irritating things. It would be easier if he was some ugly, scheming old sleaze. If his outsides matched his insides, maybe she could get some good hits in with the baseball bat and blame it on the wannabes she had chased off.

No, she could never hurt someone outside of self-defense. It was one of the tenants Andre had made sure to teach her ever since she had shown a proficiency for putting school bullies in garbage cans. There was a responsibility that came with strength, and she couldn't abuse it.

Even if the handsome, rich man was clearly coming to her home to wreck everything important to her. He wasn't the first, and unfortunately, he wasn't going to be the last.

"Probably because I am," she said.

"And why is that?"

"You know."

He leaned against the counter, flashing her a mega-watt smile that he should have to carry a license for, because it felt like a weapon, she didn't have the right comeback for. "No, I don't. You could explain it to me."

Was he... flirting with her? That wasn't right. Guys like him didn't flirt with women like her. So that just left mocking. Well, if he wanted to dish it out, she could give it back just as politely. "Because you're rich, and the rich are always greedy, right? Always wanting more, more, more, until you have everything and nobody else has anything."

That smooth expression slid from his face and he looked genuinely confused. Was she the first person to not kiss up and to tell him the truth instead?

"Is that really how you see me?"

She fixed him with the most level gaze she could. "How else should I see you?"

He didn't answer that, and she figured the conversation was done. She really wanted to get to bed. Having the handsome man in her space made her feel off-center. Like she was mad at herself for even noticing that chiseled jaw or those dark, dark, umber eyes that seemed to stare right down to her soul.

"If you head out to the desk, I'll drive your car out and we'll handle the payment and get your receipt."

"Of course," he said without any other comments.

Good. The sooner he was out of her hair, the sooner she could get in a bath and go to bed, signing off the attraction as a weird blip that she'd forget about in a couple of days.

It only took a couple of minutes to get everything all set, and then she was sliding his credit card and handing him his keys. She could practically smell the lavender bath bomb that she was going to use. They were expensive, so she didn't have many of them, but it was definitely a bath bomb sort of night.

But as she handed the man his keys, it seemed like he wanted to tell her something.

"Yes?" she asked expectantly.

"This doesn't have to be a bad process, you know. For you, your family. Or the... community." He pulled out a small square of paper from his wallet then wrote something across the back. "If you ever need anything or want to discuss what you would need to be happy with a transition, please give us a call. If my family chooses to move forward, I'm sure we can compromise. You know, do the best for everyone."

She took the card from him, glancing at it before shoving it into the pocket of her jeans.

Huh. Was he feeling guilty? Good. He should. She'd seen what happened when businesses came in, suddenly interested in low-income neighborhoods. They always built something that drove property taxes and prices up until no one could afford to live there anymore. And then all the people who lived there for years would vacate only to have the empty space snatched up by whatever wealthy folks that wanted to get in on a "promising new developmental area."

"You keep telling yourself that," she said. She didn't need to beleaguer the point. He knew how she felt and that was that. She was honest to a fault, but she felt no need to argue with him right outside her father's mechanic shop.

He didn't say anything again, although he did hesitate. With one last look at her, he got into his car and finally drove away. As he disappeared, she couldn't help but hope it was the last she would see of him.

But she also knew it was only going to get worse. The sharks were circling her home, and it would be only a matter of time before they got hungry.

6

———

Theodora

"Ah, my *habibi*, I thought I would never see you again!"

Teddy laughed as the *very* old man pressed a gentle kiss to her hand. Mr. Abadi was one of her favorites to visit. He was a charismatic man, and although he was both widowed and confined to his chair, he always was so bright whenever she visited him.

"I just saw you over the weekend," she said as she placed her basket full of veggies into his fridge. It had taken a while, but his home health aide for the past two years was excellent at making sure the bounty went to good use.

"Ah yes, but that was days ago. When you get to be as old as I am, you never know how many you'll have."

"Aw, don't play the old man card now. We both know you're going to live forever just to spite everyone who said you couldn't."

"Ah, she knows me so well! Come, sit for a minute. Read to me the paper?"

Teddy finished up what she was doing and crossed to him to kiss the top of his head. "Sorry, not today. I have to make sure I get the rest of these to Mrs. Sanchez and Routier."

"Ah, beautiful and so generous. What would we old folks ever do without you and your magic garden?"

"It's not magic, and I'm no angel."

"Hmmm, I think maybe you're wrong."

"You think whatever you want, Mr. Abadi. I'll be back on the weekend, and I'll read whatever papers you like and make you lemonade."

"Ah! Lemonda! Frieda tries to make it like you, but it's not the same."

"That's because she doesn't put a splash of lime juice in it."

"What's this? Should you be revealing such valuable secrets to me?"

She teasingly stuck her tongue out at him as she started to shut the door. "What, it's not like you're going to remember this tomorrow, old man."

He let out a loud laugh and jokingly threw a magazine. It didn't reach, of course, but Teddy blew a raspberry before closing the door completely. He was such a sweet man. She should see about getting him into the reading program for seniors at the local school. She bet a bunch of the kids would love him.

She started making a list of older folks who could be good for the program that was supposed to start over the summer. Some of them were too weak or not social enough to want to join, but for some of them, it'd be real good.

That thought perked her up as she made the rest of her

deliveries. Roman never understood why she wanted to spend so much of what little free time she had running produce across their neighborhood, but it was cathartic for her. Her way of giving back to the place and people who had been there for her in the darkest of times. Besides, she grew way more produce than she could ever get Andre and Roman to eat, so might as well not let it go to waste.

Wednesdays were her light day, where she went into the shop at noon instead of at open, so she only ran three to four deliveries. That was hardly any work at all, unlike her full day off where she ran close to ten deliveries and was out from sunup to sundown.

She headed back home, whistling as she rode along on her bike. The sun was bright, there was a nice breeze going, and she felt *good*. None of her regulars were sick or had fallen, and she had gotten a full night's sleep after a long soak in her tub. It had all the fixings of a good day, and she was ready to go into the shop and work.

Then again, she was about an hour ahead of schedule. She could go visit her mom. It'd been a while and Teddy was sure that she missed her.

Nodding to herself, she changed her course and headed toward the edge of their little neighborhood, where the church was and then the deadlands that were full of condemned buildings and abandoned businesses. A terrible fire had struck in the nineties; the area had never recovered.

But she wasn't heading for the deadlands. No, she had a different location in mind entirely.

She arrived without incident, chaining her bike to the rack at the church then crossing behind it to a large, sprawling plot of land. The church had all that land only because the holy building was so old. She was happy about it, though; the plot had several weeping willows in it and flowered bushes around the edges.

She couldn't think of a nicer graveyard for her mother to rest in.

Teddy had long since memorized the path to her mother's final resting place. Sitting down in front of it, she looked at the worn stone. She hadn't brought flowers this time, but she was sure her mother understood.

Her mother had always understood everything.

"Hey, sorry it's been a while. Things have been crazy at the shop, you know."

Mom didn't say anything, because she never did, but Teddy still felt that familiar warmth in her chest. She could see in her mind how her mom would smile and nod, reaching out her hand to hold. Was there a more welcoming place than being in the arms of her mother?

No, probably not. But that place was long gone, so all she had was the gravestone.

"I know you'd want me to get out more. You always worried about me being so serious. But I... I'm worried, Mom. There's been three different upper-echelon folks sharkin' around here. Real bloodhounds, sniffing everywhere they can get their noses. We all know what they're doing, but it scares me, ya know?"

Her mother would nod and have a solution. Mom always knew how to solve every puzzle.

Except maybe the one on getting better.

"I don't know what would happen to me if we lost this neighborhood. It's my whole life. And what if they do something to this church? What if they take *you* away? I know..." Teddy shook her head, bringing her knees up so she could rest her brow against it. "I know you're not *really* there, but this is *our* place. Just me and you. Sometimes this feels like the only place in the world where I can still feel you beside me.

"I'm scared, I guess. And angry. I just want to take all of these guys and throw them headfirst into trash cans. It's where—"

She was cut off as her phone rang. No one ever really called her unless it was about the shop, so she picked it up and answered. Mom would understand.

Teddy expected an update about a car, or a part, or a problem fix, but instead it was Jamal's panicked voice on the other end. She could hardly understand him, but what she did catch horrified her down to her core.

Swearing, she bid her goodbye to Mom and raced to her bike.

Oh no.

Her brain was blindly panicked as she peddled furiously. Her heart was in her throat and she knew she was going to have the worst thigh-burn, but that didn't matter. No. She just needed to get home as fast as possible.

Somehow, she made it without passing out, but her arrival brought no relief. She recognized the man standing in front of their shop, a ruthless businessman, a real sleazeball that they'd had issues with for a while. Oh sure, things had started out civil, but once Andre had made it clear that he wasn't interested in selling the property, things had declined rapidly.

The man wasn't alone either. His muscle was there, with a couple men in suits who she guessed were lawyers. Geez, he really was putting the pressure on, wasn't he?

Too bad that wasn't going to work. Her brother Roman was standing at the door, arms folded across his barrel chest. He had that placid look on his face that both he and Teddy had learned from Andre. If there was anyone who knew how to weather the storm, it was their dad.

"Hey," Teddy said, running up and standing beside him. She was covered in sweat, and she was acutely aware of how red her face was and how frizzy her hair was, but she didn't care. They were a united front against these interlopers. They were *family* and would present themselves as one. "I came as soon as I heard."

"Aw, it's alright," Roman said with a shrug. "Mr. Cartwright was just heading out."

"Actually, that's not quite true," the man said with a grin that really did make the shark metaphor seem that much more apt. "You see, we understand how important the community is here, and we understand where our last offer didn't really value that properly. So, we've come to offer you something that we think would be much more your speed."

"Our speed is not interested," Teddy said sharply. "We're real sorry you wasted your time comin' out here, but as we said before, this is a family business, and we plan on staying around as long as our family keeps on going."

The man narrowed his eyes. He had been so smooth, so oiled when he'd first shown up nearly six months earlier, but it was clear he was losing patience. "We understand that change can be scary, but we hope that you'll share our excitement with all the new opportunities—"

Teddy was so very tired of it all. This guy had interrupted her time with her mom, just another wrong in a long list of them. "The only thing we want to share with you is a pleasant goodbye. Thank you so much for your time, Mr. Cartwright, but you and your... employees can head back to wherever it is you came from."

"While I respect your love of this neighborhood, you're not the owner here. If I could speak to Mr. Parker—"

"He's already spoken to you and expressed his wishes. Us, his *children*, are happy to remind you of that."

"His child," the man corrected idly.

Teddy stiffened, her spine locking vertebra by vertebra. "What was that?"

"I said his child, as in his *son*. Not an informally adopted daughter who was passed off by a con artist who happened to get a pitiable disease."

Teddy saw red.

The world expanded outward, her vision going tunneled as his words reverberated in her head. She *was* Andre's daughter. He had been the only father that she had ever known. His hands had been the ones to wipe away her tears. It'd been him who taught her how to ride a bike, had taken her into a store to buy her first feminine products after her period had surprised her at the ripe ol' age of eleven. He was the one who had gone to all of her softball games, who had bandaged her hurts, had taught her everything she knew about cars. He was her *dad*.

And her mother wasn't a con artist. She was kind. She was so sweet and warm. She had never yelled at Teddy. She had only ever wanted to love and be loved. She—

Suddenly the man was stumbling back, a sickening crack splitting the air. He had been punched. And it was only after a ragged breath that Teddy realized it was Roman who had slugged him across his face.

"Don't talk to my *sister* like that!" he snarled, his face drawn up into a furious expression.

Teddy blinked, surprised by the act. She was always the scrapper, the one with the bad temper. It was so jarring to see her brother act violently, that she just stood there a moment as pandemonium erupted around her.

The muscle guys were surging forward. She yanked her brother back, putting her body in front of him and raising her fists. Sure, maybe the hired goons would have no problem attacking a black guy who slugged their boss, but she was smaller than them and a white woman, and they'd be striking her in broad daylight. She was aware of the stark difference those two scenarios carried, and she was more than fine using her body to protect her brother. Her very *real* brother, no matter what poisonous things Mr. Cartwright said.

One of the lawyers was yelling at them, but she wasn't listening. She was trying to crowd Roman backward into the shop, but he was pressing against her, still wanting to get at the men. When was the last time she'd ever seen him so incensed? She couldn't even remember.

Someone was on the phone; she was sure she heard them calling the cops. No, no, *no.* That was never good.

There was more screaming, more crowding, her holding her hands up to keep the hired guards at bay but also her legs trying to ground her to press her brother back. It was all so much. She wished Andre was there. She wished her *mom* was there.

The minutes all blended into each other, panicked and fueled with adrenaline. The cops arrived *way* too soon, as if they had been waiting close by. Like someone had tipped them off of something happening long before Mr. Cartwright had arrived. The next thing Teddy knew, her brother was being arrested and driven away, her ears rushing as the business posse all left in victory.

What had just happened? Since when was she so... so... *helpless?*

She didn't know. Her brain was spinning. She wasn't even aware that anyone was talking to her until someone gripped her arm and yanked her into the shop.

She shoved back, alarmed and confused, coming back to reality to realize it was Hassan, who was holding out a water bottle to her and ordering her to drink. She did, realizing her hands were shaking.

What had just happened?

"We called your father. He's on his way. You need to breathe, okay? Just breathe, *chica*, we all got you. Your brother is gonna be okay."

Breathe. Drink. Drink. Breathe.

It had just been a normal day. A *good* day. How had everything gone so wrong so fast? Had they been set up?

It felt like that, but that thought was also too terrifying to think about. There was blood in the water now, and the sharks were growing more and more desperate. How could her family fight them? The sharks had time, money and the smarts. All her community had was each other, and what was that if they were picked off one by one. A fight here. A disturbance there. It was no secret that most of the cops weren't overly fond of her area, especially with the gangs. They would probably be all too happy to come clear out such a 'troubled' area. What was there to be done? She couldn't just roll over and give in. There was too much at stake. But was fighting them just suicide?

"Sweet pea? You okay? I'm here. I'm here now."

Teddy looked up with watery eyes to see her dad standing in the door of the shop, looking as worried and scared as she felt. She didn't have to think twice as she threw herself at him, and his strong arms wrapped around her. Hugging her. Holding her. He was her rock. Her comfort. He had protected her all these years, and she loved him so much.

"It's okay. It's gonna be okay, Teddy. I'm going to go to the police station. If you want to come with me, I'm going to need you to breathe and pull yourself together. They can't see us weak. You know how it is."

Teddy nodded, letting the warm rise and fall of his chest dictate her own breath. She could be calm for her brother. She could pack everything away until it was okay to feel again.

"Let's go get Roman," she said.

"That's my girl."

He pressed a kiss to her forehead and then they were rushing out, jumping into the beater of a car he drove around and heading to the station. The entire time, Teddy worked on composing herself. She couldn't afford to lose her temper. She couldn't be some hysterical woman making a scene. Besides, maybe if she was pitiable enough, personable enough, they would believe that Roman was acting in self-defense.

Which wasn't technically true. He'd been acting in *her* defense. But they were family and that was almost the same thing... right?

They reached the police station before she really had an answer and then they were going in. Everything was kinda hazy, most details rushing past her as she looked around for her brother. Had they already taken his fingerprints? Admitted him? Was that even the right word? She had no idea.

It seemed to take forever to find the right person to talk to, and once they did, a cop intercepted them and proceeded to give them the worst time. His comments were snide, his directions were vague, and the two of them had to sit there and take it. To smile and placate and be as polite as possible while the man they were talking to exaggerated Roman's actions like he was a hardened criminal.

But the end of the conversation rocked her world. The cop

explained that Roman was being booked and that he was being held for a full forty-eight hours before his arraignment. No discussion. No wiggle room.

Her brother was going to be in jail for two days.

Teddy just stared forward, and for the first time in a long while, she felt so utterly defeated. Was there a way out from the hole they had suddenly found themselves in?

It certainly didn't feel like it.

7

Silas

"Hand me that scrubber, would ya? There's a bit of corrosion packed in here."

"You know that's not what it's called, right."

Silas shot his older brother a look. "Oh really, Solomon? And what would you like me to call it then?"

Solomon laughed as he handed him the bristled tool. "Honestly, I don't even remember. Here you go."

Silas took it happily, cleaning around an area that was packed with debris and rust. He would need to oil it once he was done—which surprisingly was probably going to be that day.

He hadn't had any plans when he'd woken up—grateful to be done collecting all of the information that his dad wanted about the new development. His older brother had approached him and asked if he wanted to help work on the feed grinder.

And the strange thing was, Silas had agreed. Sterling was off with their dad to a business thing because it was his turn. People could rarely tell them apart, so the two of them hardly ever attended events at the same time. Some folks apparently thought this meant that Dad only had five sons, but Silas thought that was hilarious.

"You know, we have workers who we literally pay to do this," Silas commented absently, finishing using the scrubber and reaching for the oil rag they had been using.

"Yeah, but it's kinda nice to do something with our hands, isn't it?"

There was something odd about his tone. Almost wistful? Melancholy? The elder twin couldn't place his finger on it, but he was acutely aware that *something* was changing with his brother.

Could it be that city girl?

His brother had always been so stern, so dedicated to the business; it seemed impossible that just one person could change him in any way.

"It is," Silas agreed eventually. "Not that we're very good at it. If Dad wasn't so fit to be tied about Samuel, maybe we could just fly Benji here to teach us. Except Dad would never agree to that."

Solomon paused in what they were doing, looking at all the tools they had laid out around them, the two manuals being held open with clamps, and the mess they'd created. "Hah, I suppose not. But it's getting done, isn't it?"

Silas cracked another smile. "Yeah. It is. Wanna go for a ride with me after this?"

"You've been hanging around the stables a lot. Anything going on there?"

"Just reconnecting with some of the things we used to do a lot more of when we were younger."

"You mean before Dad got into that fight with our uncle and then went real obsessed with 'building his legacy'?"

Now it was Silas' turn to pause, and he did, giving his brother a long look. "Is that what happened?"

"You were real young. You probably don't remember. Probably didn't even realize that things were changing right away either."

Silas didn't know what to think about that, but before he could say anything, his phone was buzzing. Taking off one of his gloves, he pulled it from his pocket. It was his twin, Sterling.

Mrs. Worthington called me Silas three times today. This is hilarious. I'm going to make you look like such a jerk.

Silas chuckled to himself, knowing that his twin was teasing. He wouldn't damage any of their reputations purposefully because none of them would ever hear the end of it from their dad.

Don't you dare, Silas texted back quickly. He did feel bad that his brother was stuck at a tedious sort of charity event that was less about giving back to the poor and was more about the political machinations of their dad. He loved his dad; he really

did. But he couldn't help but feel that certain things were...
wrong? No, that wasn't the right word for it.

Too late. I already spiked the punch bowl.

You're juvenile.

Thank you, I do try.

You're just doing this so Dad will never ask you to another event.

Stop twin-reading my mind.

Stop being so obvious.

*Yeah, yeah. Whatever, time to go drown myself in the punch bowl
before I have to deal with another debutante here hitting on me but
thinking I'm you. You owe me.*

Love you too, little brother.

Only by ten minutes!

.   .   .

SILAS CHUCKLED and tucked his phone away. When he returned to his work, he saw Solomon eyeing him curiously.

"Something up?" Silas asked.

Solomon shrugged and then shook his head. "That Sterling?"

"Who else would it be?"

"Right. It's not like any of us talk to anyone outside the family."

Now *that* was bitter. It surprised Silas, and he found himself looking over his older brother again. So many things were changing, but they were such small things that Silas wasn't sure what to think about any of it.

"Hey, you okay, brother?" Silas asked.

Solomon shrugged yet again; his mouth pulled into something that was possibly supposed to be a smile but was just his lips pressed into a very thin, tight line. It was the kind of grin that wasn't a grin at all, but rather a sarcastic expression to communicate that no, he wasn't okay in the slightest. "Why wouldn't I be?"

Silas chose his next words carefully. He had been harboring thoughts for a while, sure. Uncertainty even. But it was another thing entirely to voice them to the heir of his dad's empire. The so-called leader of the next generation.

And yet, he found his mouth opening and words were slowly slipping out.

"Have you ever wanted more than what Dad sees for us?"

There, they were out, and they hung there, heavy in the air. An accusation, a question, a worry. All of them and none of them. Silas felt the skin along his arms and the back of his neck prickle. He was never one to rock the boat. He made evaluations and did what his dad asked of him. He was smart, but not smart enough to be a decision man.

Solomon was quiet again, for an impossible time before he cleared his throat. "Why do you ask that?"

Ugh. That was not a good answer. Silas hadn't lived twenty-eight years on the earth to not know what that was. "Ah, nothing. Just one of those thought exercises from online. Never mind. It wasn't important."

But Solomon's jaw was tensing like he wasn't dismissing it at all. Silas tried to return to working, wishing he had never said anything. But then it was his brother who was speaking, much to his surprise.

"Honestly? Yes. Lately, it seems to me that we've become a lot more like the Pharisees in the Bible and a whole lot less like Jesus."

Oh.

That was... something Silas had not expected.

At all.

He swallowed, his gaze flicking up to his brother before returning to the tools scattered around him. "That's a pretty heavy charge there. Being some of the bad guys of the Bible."

"I know. But I'm trying to figure out how to change it."

"Is that why the tension has been amping up between you and Dad lately?"

"Has it?" Solomon answered drolly. "I hadn't noticed."

"Right. Well, uh, good luck with that."

"Thanks, Silas. And let's... let's keep this conversation between the two of us. Brother to brother."

"Yeah," Silas said, breathing shakily. "That sounds like a good idea."

Solomon nodded, and then they were back to work. Silas tried to let the matter go, to return to the contentment that he had been feeling from working with his hands. But his mind kept returning to what his brother had said.

Teddy clearly saw his family as the bad guys. Those gang members had. And now his own brother. How many people could share the same opinion without it being true?

And if it was true, where did that leave Silas?

8

Theodora

Teddy woke up from a haze of nightmares, soaked in sweat and feeling like she hadn't rested at all. With a grumble, she kicked off her mountain of blankets and headed for the bathroom.

Normally she was a night showerer, using the spray to rinse away the trials and dirt of the day so she could slip into bed for a refreshing sleep. But she felt both clammy and overheated, her head spinning from the last of her dreams that were fading from her memory with every moment.

It was the day of her brother's arraignment. She was going to see her brother again. She hadn't gone two full days without seeing him in years, and she missed him. She worried about him. What if Mr. Cartwright had arranged for something to happen while he was behind bars?

That thought made her stomach churn and she paused in

front of the toilet, wondering if she was going to be sick. Why did Roman have to punch the guy? He had been protecting her, but she wasn't worth it. She wasn't worth any of it.

No use thinking that. What was done was done, and she needed to get dressed and out of the house before she went insane.

Teddy went about her morning routine robotically, not allowing herself to think. But when she headed toward the kitchen to brew herself some coffee, she was surprised to see that a full breakfast was waiting for her.

"Hey there, sweet pea," Andre said, already sitting at the table and sipping a cup of coffee. "How're you feeling?"

"About how you'd expect," she said with a sigh, crossing to the coffee pot. "You were up early to make all of this."

"Well, I guess you could say that I was having trouble sleeping."

She nodded and sat across from him at the table. "I get that." She looked over the food, but she couldn't hide the frown on her face.

"What's wrong, sweet pea?"

"I... I think I'm too upset to eat. I feel like I have rocks in my stomach."

"Fair enough. You know I made all this, and I couldn't so much as get a pancake down."

There was a quiver to his wan smile and Teddy reached across the table, intertwining her fingers with his. They were old digits, long with thick knuckles, callouses built on top of callouses. They were the fingers that had helped care for her for fourteen years.

"How about we pack up enough to feed Roman once he's released and put the rest in the fridge? I bet they ain't giving him square meals in there," Teddy said.

Andre smiled gratefully, his white teeth striking against his umber skin. "That's an idea. Let's do that."

She nodded, and together they tried to act like everything was normal as the minutes ticked away. As it were, they still headed out obnoxiously early, neither of them willing to wait in the house a moment longer. Just a couple more hours, and they would be reunited again. Her family would be safe.

Relatively.

They made it to the courthouse in good time, but Teddy had never expected to get hung up in the metal detector line. First of all, both of the lines were painfully slow, with the machines giving off false beeps and people seeming to forget that they were wearing metal jewelry or a belt. But when it finally got to her and Andre, it seemed like the thing would not stop going off.

"Do you have any metal on your person?" one of the guards asked.

"*No*," Teddy answered for the third time, her arms extended from her sides as the officer scanned her with one of those wand-things.

"Are you sure, ma'am? Piercings? Even wire in your bra could set these off."

Teddy bit her tongue. She'd gone through metal detectors plenty and knew enough to wear a sports bra. She'd learned that lesson in high school when she'd attempted to wear something fancy to be like one of the popular girls, but the size of the support in her underthings had set off the detector again and again until she'd had to have a pat-down by a school counselor.

"No, I have no piercings, not even my ears, and I'm not wearing an underwire."

"Alright, ma'am. I'm still getting a positive here."

"That's so strange," Teddy remarked dryly, looking over to Andre, who was receiving similar treatment. "Especially since it keeps beeping at a different area of my body every time."

"What was that?"

Teddy affixed the blandest look that she could onto her face. "I noticed your thumb is by a very distinct button on the side. Could it be that you're accidentally brushing the test-button as you move? I once did the same thing with one of my readers on a car I was working on. I was *so* embarrassed."

The officer was quiet for a very long moment, giving her a hard look. She just continued smiling on blithely like she wasn't accusing him of anything. Which she most definitely was. She was just smart about it.

"Oh, maybe that's what's happening. Let me try that." He changed his grip on the wand and, what a surprise, it didn't beep. "Well, would you look at that. You can gather your things and go, ma'am."

"Thanks. And would you be a darling and check if your coworker is accidentally doing the same thing to my father?" She kept it saccharine. Sweet. She could play the part if she had to; she just tried not to most of the time.

The guard looked from her to Andre and back, and she could see the dozens of thoughts flitting behind his eyes. "Your father?"

"Yes, father. Why do you ask?"

"Uh, no reason. I'll go do that."

"Thanks. I appreciate you more than you know."

The guard walked off and soon enough, she and Andre were finally able to move on, shoving their things hastily into their pockets as they headed toward the elevator.

"How much time did that waste?" Andre grumbled, looking like he was holding back his irritation.

"Forty-five minutes," Teddy answered him, trying to pull back the bite in her tone. "But it's alright. We're still early."

"Yeah, good thing we left when we did." He cleared his throat. "I've got a bad feeling about this."

"You're not the only one," Teddy muttered under her breath. She had this feeling that the incident with the metal detectors was not an accident. But acknowledging that it wasn't had a whole bunch of very scary implications that she didn't want to think about. Like how much power the Cartwright man might have or how big the business he represented actually was.

They finally reached the elevator they had been directed to and headed up, but when they exited and approached another choke point where a worker was, she had that same feeling of something being wrong again.

"We're here for the arraignment of Roman Parker."

The woman looked down at her list, flipping through a couple pages, her brow furrowing until she made a clicking noise with her tongue.

"I'm sorry, but that was bumped to earlier today. That ended about twenty minutes ago."

Teddy stared at her. "What? What happened? What do we even do now?"

"Take the elevator down two floors. There will be a clerk who will tell you what his bail has been set at and arrange for payment of it."

"Really? Another line?"

"I think you'll find we have a lot of those here," the woman said, flashing them a smile. Teddy could tell that she was trying to use humor to ease the situation, but it didn't really work.

"Thanks," she managed to say not too bitterly, and then it was off to yet another line.

It didn't take long for them to find where they were supposed to go, but there was a long, *long* stretch of people all standing there, looking like they were in various stages of stress.

Oh great.

Teddy spoke up, "Hey, so this is going to take longer than we thought. Why don't you go move the car or pay the meter again, and I'll take care of this?"

"You sure?" Andre asked, looking like he was getting more and more flustered. "That'll take a while. Especially if they give me trouble on re-entry again."

Teddy flashed him a crooked smile. "Oh, don't worry. I'm not under any illusion that this'll be quick."

He looked to the long line then back to her before nodding appreciatively. "Alright then. Sounds like a plan. I'll be back."

"I'll be here," she said, heaving a sigh. "I'll definitely be here."

He went off and she took her place at the end of the line, pulling her phone out. Unfortunately, there was hardly any reception at all, so even just looking at memes or social media was taking ages. Not exactly enough to distract her from all of the stress and worry building in her middle.

It was hard to say exactly how much time passed by, especially since she had her thumb over the clock on her phone so she wouldn't keep staring at it. But Andre was still gone by the time she made it to the front of the line. They must have been giving him a *real* hard time at the metal detector.

Ugh.

But it was easy enough to hand over her ID and explain who she was looking for and that she wanted to pay his bail. If the woman thought anything about her stating their familiar relation, she didn't say so. But that was probably because she was saying something completely impossible.

"Roman Parker's bail has been set at five hundred thousand dollars. Will you be paying that with check or debit?"

Teddy blinked at her. Then blinked some more. "I'm sorry, *what?*"

"Roman Parker's bail has been set at five hundred thousand dollars. How would you like to pay for that? If you would like to put something else up as collateral, we will need you to come back."

Teddy continued to stare at her, feeling like the world was spinning off in impossible directions. "I'm sorry… you're telling me that my brother's bail is set at *half a million dollars?*"

"Yes, that is correct. Do you still wish to put up for his release?"

Teddy didn't answer her, instead stumbling away, her mind rushing.

Five hundred thousand dollars.

One half of a million.

What?

She stood there in the middle of things, just staring, feeling like she was sputtering out and that she needed to be jump-started. What the hell was going on!? That couldn't be true. What had her brother even been charged with?

"Oh, fancy seeing you here, Ms. Parker."

The unfortunately familiar voice drew her attention. She forced herself back to reality to see Smarmy McSmarmer right in front of her, otherwise known as Mr. Cartwright.

"What are you doing here?" she ground out, her fists curling at her sides. She wanted to punch him; she really did.

But she'd at least learned enough from what was happening with her brother not to do that.

But he waved the question away with his long, spindly hand. "Does it matter?" he said with a grin before continuing on. "I couldn't help but overhear what happened at that window. You know, this has all been such a mess. I hate to see a family taken apart, so how about I just take care of the bail for you?"

It felt like every cell in Teddy's body jumped at once, and she had to school her features to stay neutral. "And what would you want in return?"

"Who said I would want anything at all?"

"People like you don't give away a half a million dollars for free."

He laughed—an oily, gross sound that made Teddy's skin crawl. She wanted to take a shower again, if only to cleanse herself of his greed. "Fair enough. I think a fair trade would be your family signing over the property. Then, once the trial's all wrapped up, you can keep the refund of the bail and we'll all go our separate ways, right as rain."

Of course.

Of *freaking* course.

Teddy's temper ramped up again. "You conniving snake of a man," she hissed so gutturally she wasn't surprised when he shot her a confused look.

"I'm sorry, what was that?"

She took a step closer, keeping her hands down but crowding his chest. She didn't care that he was taller than her. "I said you *conniving snake of a man*," she spat even louder. "You set us up, and now you think you can sweep in and manipulate us so your greedy little fingers can snatch up everything you wanted."

The man swallowed, his eyes flicking about uncertainly, like he had thought she was too dumb to catch his obvious ruse. "Need I remind you it was *your* brother who hit me."

"Don't play the victim. You insulted my dead mother and me on our family property. And now you're using all the connections you have with all your other fellow rats to try to win. But you won't. You don't have half of what you need to take on me and my family. You can manipulate and twist and lie and bribe, but we're not gonna fold to you or anyone like you. You got that?"

Her finger was poking into his chest, and he was staring down at her with a mix of frustration and maybe something else. Fear? Respect? Incredulousness? It didn't matter.

"Look, I understand you might be overly emotional right now," he said, seeming to recover. He reached into his pocket, and the next thing she knew, he was sliding a card into her curled hand. "Why don't you process things, and then call me when that pride of yours simmers down."

She pulled her lips back from her teeth as if she were going to snarl, but he was already walking away, back to his usual swagger, which *really* made her want to deck him.

But she didn't. Instead, her phone rang. She answered it, her father's voice crackling from the poor reception.

"Hey, they wouldn't let me in, so I brought the car around. Is everything handled? Do you have Roman?"

"I..." She looked down at the card in her hand and swallowed. "There's been a delay. You should go on back home and make sure everything's going good at the shop. I'll take care of things here."

"Are you sure? You can't be having fun in there."

"I'm not. But if you're stuck outside, you might as well keep yourself occupied."

"Fair enough, sweet pea. Let me know if anything comes up. I'll head back up here after I get a few things done at the shop."

"Of course. Love you, Dad."

"Love you too."

She hung up and shoved her phone into her pocket. But as she did, she felt something else in there. Pulling it out, she saw it was the business card of that handsome, rich man whose car she had fixed. She'd forgotten entirely about it and almost about him with everything that had been happening.

Huh... he had said if her family ever needed anything...

No. That was just trading one shark for another. Just because he was pretty didn't mean he didn't want to dismantle everything she loved.

Then again... did she really have a choice?

9

—————

Silas

Silas was in the middle of helping Mom sow her late seedlings in her garden when his personal cell phone rang. He could count on one hand the number of people who had access to that information, so he looked at his phone curiously.

It was an unknown number, but local. What did that mean?

He stopped working to answer the call. Sure, curiosity might have killed the cat, but at least satisfaction had brought it back.

"Hello?" he asked curiously.

"Hi. Mr. Miller?"

It was a woman's voice. For some reason that surprised him, along with the fact that he somewhat recognized it. A sort of vague familiarity that tugged at the back of his brain but offered no actual information.

"Who is this?"

"Teddy. Teddy Parker."

"Teddy Parker?"

"From the mechanic shop. The baseball bat?"

"Ted—*oh*. Ms. Parker. Hello." Why on earth was she calling him? And not from the mechanic shop phone either. "How ca—"

"Did you mean what you said about things not having to be awful? About a... a *compromise*?"

Silas didn't answer for a moment, his brain trying to catch up. "What do you mean by that?"

"Just come to the courthouse in the city. I'll explain everything when you get here."

And then she hung up.

That was... that was not what he expected. Was he suddenly in some sort of espionage movie? He didn't think so. Why would he go into the city when the woman had pretty much had no compunction telling him how little she thought of him? She hadn't even been very polite, and *she* was the one that called *his* phone.

"Hey honey, what's going on? Does your dad need something?"

Silas looked to his mother, where she was kneeling in the dirt on the chunk of her garden reserved for seedlings that needed to be planted later in the spring and at the cusps of summer. They were having a nice time together, and he didn't really want to leave her...

"No, but there's something I need to do in the city. I'll see you later tonight, okay?"

"Of course, dear. Drive safely. I'll have plenty to do tomorrow if you want to join me."

He smiled at her, wiping his hands on his thighs. He could smell the fresh earth and greenery all around them, with the faintest hint of different herbs just starting to reach maturity. It was a good combination, and one that made him feel welcome. At home.

"Yeah, Mom. That sounds nice."

It took longer than he liked to get to the courthouse. Traffic was abysmal, and the parking was worse. He wasn't sure where to meet the woman, but his question was answered when he spotted her figure standing on the steps, arms crossed and her posture stiff as she paced.

He strode toward her quickly, but his rate slowed when his eyes were able to pick out more details of her.

She wasn't in her normal mechanic's jumpsuit, instead wearing a formal-looking dress in a pretty, powder blue and nude wedges on her feet. Her red hair was up in a bun, with that one bleached streak at her temple making a stark stripe through the bright, coppery color.

She looked *stunning*, like a classic pinup girl, except with bigger biceps and a softer frame, generous curves and muscles all packaged up together to make a real lovely picture.

But then he saw the expression on her face and all those thoughts fled his head. She did *not* look happy. What was wrong?

Her eyes finally landed on him, and the look of relief that crossed her features made him wonder what exactly was going on.

"You came," she said, walking quickly toward him. "I didn't think you would."

"I gave you my card for a reason. I'm glad you called."

"Right. Right." She looked over her shoulder as if she was worried about someone watching them, then quickly strode forward to close the distance between them. She linked her arm through his, then pulled him along. "There's a nice area with benches we can walk to. Let's go there. Away from here."

"Sure. Whatever you want."

Silas thought she was acting very mysterious. A new vulnerability replaced her cold demeanor from the shop. Mainly, though, he couldn't get over how different—how beautifully feminine—she looked in her dress and heels. He didn't want to pay attention to it, especially considering how upset she looked, but he also felt like he couldn't help it at the same time.

She let go of him when they reached the area that she had been talking about. It was an almost promenade-like area with trees on either side and plenty of benches overlooking a park just across the street. But she didn't start talking right away, instead crossing her arms again and beginning to pace.

"Hey, what's wrong?" Silas asked.

She looked at him, then her eyes slid away, then back to him again. "My brother got into some trouble."

"Oh?" What else would he say to that?

"One of your friends, or maybe even a business rival, who knows, came to our home and played us. He set us up, and now he's trying to force our hand and have us sign over our property to get Roman out of trouble."

The words tumbled out of her mouth, one right after the other, and it was about the opposite of how she had been that night with the baseball bat. Its juxtaposition was a little off-putting, but he did his best to listen.

"Whoa, slow down. What's going on?"

She took a deep breath. "There's a man who's been trying to snatch up our property. He goaded my brother into a fight and now my brother's in jail. They want a half a million dollars for his bail. We can't afford that, but Cartwright said if we sign our business over, he'll cover it.

"But we're not going to sign over our business. We can't. But I also can't let my brother rot in jail until his trial. It's clear that shark has connections in there, and who knows what he'll do to Roman. So, I *need* that five hundred thousand dollars, but he knows I have no way of getting it."

Silas kept quiet a moment while his brain caught up with the moment. "Are you asking me to give you half a million dollars?"

Her face went pale and the look that crossed her features was heartbreaking. "No! I mean... yes. I suppose that's the long and the short of it. I... I shouldn't have called. This was a dumb idea."

She turned to go, but he caught her arm. "Wait, no, I offered to help. I'm just trying to understand everything. What I'm getting is that your brother has a high bail and you think—wait. Did you say *Cartwright*? As in Philip Cartwright?"

"I don't know his first name actually."

Silas felt his brain piecing things together. Philip Cartwright was the third son of his dad's frenemy, if either of the old men would ever admit to something like that. Their businesses tended to run adjacent to each other, and more often than not, they ended up getting into a bidding war on property. But if Cartwright was around... well, that didn't bode well.

"If he's willing to pay off a half a mil' for y'all, then that means he's more than interested in your property."

"Oh yeah, he's interested. Although sometimes I think that half of it is that we shut him down so hard and hurt his pride."

"To be honest, I'd rather pay it off for you than have his fingers in it."

Her eyebrows raised. "Wow. He has to be pretty slimy if he's a sleaze among the other sharks."

"Is that what you see me as? A shark?"

She swallowed then glanced away from him. "What if... what if it wasn't you just paying it off. What if it was more... an investment in our business?"

"An investment?"

"Yeah, you pay this and I'll, uh, I can provide mechanical help for anything on your ranch. Andre taught me most everything I know, and I've got several certifications in other heavy mechanics besides cars."

"Really? You get tractors in your shop often?"

"No," she answered quickly, honestly. "But I graduated a year early, so I went to the local tech school and got every certification they had. Then I went to an apprenticeship for a while up north. Andre was willing to pay for me to stay up there a few more years, but I wanted to come back home, so I did."

"Heavy machinery then?"

"Yeah. Tractors, trailers, threshers. A large smattering of equipment. I could be real helpful. Normally a specialist costs close to thirty dollars an hour salaried and about forty-five when they're on call or freelance, so you'd have me for a couple years or so."

Now Silas was the one who was pacing. He hadn't expected to come to the city and basically be offered an indentured servant sort of situation.

It wasn't that five hundred thousand was a *lot* of money. He'd spent that much before. But it was a lot of money to just *give* to someone, even if they were offering their mechanical expertise.

"You know, the easiest solution would be to let me buy out your father's business and be done with all of this."

"No. Absolutely not. We're not selling out. So it's either make a deal with me now or let this Cartwright fellow string up my brother like some sort of scarecrow."

"You wouldn't give in even to save your brother?"

"You think my brother wouldn't throttle me if I didn't do everything in my power to save our family's shop?"

"Right. Fair enough." He licked his lips, his heart thumping far too loudly in his chest. All of his mind was telling him not to, but that wasn't what came out of his mouth. "Alright. I'll do it."

Her eyes went wide, and she looked stunned that he had agreed. "What? Really? You will?"

He nodded. "But only if you and your father meet up with me, my brother Solomon and our lawyers to make an official contract. I want this one hundred percent legal, for both of our protection."

He watched the column of her throat as she swallowed hard, pink rising up her throat until her cheeks were flushed. "Can we keep my father out of it? Please? I really don't want him to have the stress if I can help it." Silas wasn't sure about that, but he decided he could compromise.

Besides, he was probably making a terrible choice as it were.

"So, shall we go inside and get your brother out?" he said.

"Really? You're not going to make me wait until we sign the contract?"

"You said you don't want your brother in jail, right? Well I don't either. Let's say that this is a sign of trust, between the two of us."

She nodded. "Right, some trust. I suppose we're going to need a lot of that, considering I'll be working for you for the foreseeable future."

"Yeah, ha-ha. That's right, I suppose."

And wasn't that something? He hoped that he hadn't made a really dumb business decision for no reason.

One thing for certain, his dad would absolutely flip his lid if he found out.

So Silas would have to make sure that he didn't.

Ever.

10

———————

Theodora

*I*t'd been two days since her brother came home and, so far, neither Andre nor Roman was aware of Teddy essentially signing away her soul.

Well... metaphorically.

She was sure that she had probably made the wrong choice, that she had sunk herself deeper into a trap with rich folks who were used to playing on levels that she couldn't even imagine. But she didn't see how she had any other choice. Whenever she saw her brother around their home, it made her that much more certain that her choice was the right one.

But that didn't stop the nerves in her stomach from twisting and bubbling as she headed out the door. Silas—she had thought to pay attention to his first name as he'd signed the papers to release her brother—had texted her the day previously to show up at an address to sign the contract he had talked about. She couldn't help but feel like she was walking into the lair of some sort of monster.

Which was silly, because Silas was definitely doing her a solid. And that was putting it mildly. He was essentially giving them another chance, subverting Cartwright and also giving her a chance to hone her skills that she hadn't really been able to work on since she came back home.

"Hey, where ya headed to?" Roman asked, eating the last of the leftovers from the night previous. Andre had cooked quite the spread and, while it had been delicious, her stomach had been too twisted into knots to eat more than a couple mouthfuls.

"Just out. My last morning off got interrupted."

"Ah, fair enough. Look, I'm sorry for causing all this... drama, I guess you could say."

Teddy crossed over to him and kissed the top of his head. "Thank you for everything. You don't have to apologize."

His strong arms wrapped around her and pulled her to him. "You know you're my sister, right? No ifs, ands or buts about it."

There was that warm, wonderful feeling that was always so good at reminding her that she wasn't alone, that she was exactly where she needed to be. She had done the right thing to get him out, even if it terrified her.

"Yeah, I do. I promise."

"Alright, well head out. Have fun."

"Oh yeah," she said, trying not to sound too sarcastic. "So much fun."

IT DIDN'T TAKE her too long to catch the bus and ride it down to the richer part of the city, where the businesses sort of separated the riffraff from the upper echelon. Although when she got out, she got lost trying to find the exact building.

But even with that, she arrived at a nondescript rental that looked like it was used for fancy meetings and other corporate shindigs about ten minutes earlier than she was supposed to be there. Oh well, she figured she might as well head in.

So she did, following the directions that Silas had texted her, and that was how she found herself opening a door and stepping into her official contract signing.

It felt like there should have been ominous music in the background, the kind that played whenever a character in a movie was making a choice that would doom them later. But instead, there was a polite greeting from the occupants.

Because there were occupants. As in plural. Another handsome man was standing beside Silas while a more nondescript one sat at the table with a stack of papers in front of him.

"Hello, Ms. Parker," Silas said, cracking that same charming smile. "This is my brother, Solomon, and this is our contract lawyer, Chris."

"You can call me Teddy," she said, stepping forward and shaking their hands.

"Alright then, Teddy," the lawyer said, looking professional but amiable. "Shall we get started? I'm told that you run your own business, so I'm sure your free time is quite valuable. I'll try to get through this as fast as possible."

"Thanks," she said uncertainly, waiting for the two Miller brothers to sit before she did as well. "I appreciate that."

"Of course. Now, let's get started, shall we?"

They did, and she was surprised that it actually wasn't that painful of an experience. They established what she owed and her services, as well as when she needed to be on call. She was going to be spending her full day off—Tuesday—at the ranch, doing maintenance and upgrades on their vehicles and equipment that she was familiar with. Then she was supposed to come in Sunday after she finished her deliveries, and for the other four days, she was only on call.

There were stipulations about holidays and how much she could work in a single week and things like that, but there didn't seem to be any underhanded tricks. It was a straightforward payback of the half mil that he had essentially lent her.

Sooner than she thought, they were wrapping things up, and things were gearing toward a goodbye. She was relieved, to be entirely honest, because she was on edge from being around the rich strangers.

"How is your brother doing, by the way?" Silas asked as she stood, surprising her. She hadn't expected him to care.

"Good, good. He said it was mostly boring in there."

"Well that's good."

"Oh, I was meaning to ask Ms. Par—I mean, Teddy," the lawyer said, standing as well. "Who is representing your brother?"

It took her a minute to get what he meant, and when she did, her stomach sank. "We, uh, we really haven't gotten that far. He has a public defender, last I knew."

"Ah, well, if you want to change that, I recommend you get right on that. It can take time to find the right match."

"Uh, thanks. I'm not really sure that we can afford that right now, but I'll keep it in mind."

A strange expression crossed the lawyer's face, but they nodded instead of saying anything. "Of course. I hope you have a great day, Teddy. It was great working with you." A quick glance to the brothers showed that they, too, were wearing that same dubious but polite mask.

She quickly moved her gaze away, not wanting to be caught staring. Sure, they were cute, but she didn't want to send the wrong message.

"Yeah, you too." She knew that expression meant something, but she didn't have the energy to puzzle it all out.

She had enough on her plate as it was.

11

Theodora

It was Teddy's first day on the ranch, and she was nervous.

She'd been spending far too much time nervous, but there wasn't much to do about it. She'd made a five-hundred-thousand-dollar deal behind her family's back and was trying to fulfill it while also keeping it a secret. She was also going to be spending time working on a property that was worth millions of dollars.

That was insane. Every time she thought about it, it made her nauseous all over again. But she tucked that away and steeled herself. She did what she had to do to protect her family, and that would have to be enough.

She arrived at the worker area of the ranch, having borrowed one of the junkers abandoned at their shop, and was surprised when it was none other than Silas standing there to greet her.

Except, he wasn't alone. He looked like he was standing next to... a copy of himself?

She approached uncertainly, sure that she was seeing things, but the closer she got the more she realized that yeah, they were the spitting image of each other.

Twins? Why did that seem so uncanny?

"Hey there, glad to see you made it alright," Silas said, cracking that same charming grin. "This is my brother Sterling. We wanted to make sure you got in alright. We figured we'd show you around so you could get settled in."

The other nodded. Once she was right up near them, she could tell that there were a few minute differences between them. One was ever so slightly broader, and one had a slightly darker rush of stubble. But other than that, they were both dark-haired with brown eyes so deep that they were almost pitch black. But instead of being scary, or unwelcoming, there was something captivating about those umber depths.

Actually... maybe that was scary enough in and of itself.

"Sure, yeah. Show me around. The sooner I know where everything is, the sooner I can get to work."

The copy—*Sterling*—laughed and stepped forward to offer his hand. "My brother said you were intense. I see he wasn't kidding."

"That's one of the kinder words I've heard to describe me."

They both laughed at that and wow, was it strange to hear mirth in stereo. "Alright then," Silas said, the corner of his eyes crinkling. "Let's get started."

Unsurprisingly, the area she was supposed to work in was impressive. It was a garage about three times bigger than their entire shop and tricked out with almost more tools than she knew what to do with. The ceilings were lofted, allowing for the larger vehicles and equipment to come in.

They also showed her where the bathrooms were, lockers, and a place to get some grub. She hadn't expected that part, but it was good to know that she wouldn't be screwed if she forgot her lunch.

"Alright, do you have any questions?" Silas asked once they were back at the garage.

"No," she said honestly. They'd been good guides, and once someone went over any special details, the rest was pretty easy to figure out. "So, what should I get started on?"

"You want to get to work already? Normally people try to milk their first day for at least a couple hours." That was Sterling, and the grin he cracked was bigger than his brother's, with more shining white teeth. Teddy got the feeling that he might be the more dramatic of the two.

"Well, I like to get things going. You know, idle hands and all of that."

"Ah yeah, I've heard that before."

"Well, we can get out of your hair then," Silas said, taking a step back. "Wouldn't want to get in the way of your work."

"Ah, but it is such fabulous hair," Sterling said with a wink.

Huh, so he was a flirt. Interesting considering his brother hadn't so much as hinted at anything beyond boyish charm. If she had to guess, Sterling was probably the younger one. She'd had a few twin friends growing up and half the time, the younger one would be the more gregarious to stand out from their older sibling.

"I'm not so sure about that," she said with a polite smile, looking to the nearest tool chests. Her fingers were itching to start organizing—getting things in an order that would make her workflow smoother.

Silas let out a disappointed noise and grabbed his brother's arm. "Come on, let's get going before you make her quit on her first day."

Finally, the two handsome, rich bachelors were heading away from her. Technically, she didn't know if they were bachelors or not. She was sure that they had to have at least some sort of side piece. They were practically billionaires and borderline models. There was no way they were spending their days single.

Besides, why was she even worrying about their relationship status? That was the last thing that she should care about since technically they were both her employers.

Shaking her head, she put that thought to the side and got to organizing.

Time quickly began to fly by as she went about her business, opening drawers, moving things around, rearranging what was by which power outlets. Especially around the half of the garage that had the lifts. She liked certain tools to be by those and in the wells, with others where the larger equipment would be brought in.

She was so into her work that she nearly jumped when a knock sounded on one of the half-open garage doors and she spun, wrench in hand.

She wasn't sure who to expect, but it certainly wasn't a young woman with wildly colored hair. "Hey there, sorry to startle you," she said with a drawl. "I was just wondering if you would like to come eat lunch."

"Who are you?" Teddy asked uncertainly. She certainly wasn't dressed like a worker. She had old-fashioned, high waisted shorts on, multi-colored tights and a pastel camisole.

She was quite tanned, with cat eyeliner making her hazel eyes look mysterious.

"Oh, name's Frenchie. I'm kinda seeing Solomon, the oldest brother here. He mentioned you were around, and I figured I wouldn't mind a lady friend to come eat lunch with me in the big manor."

Teddy blinked at her. *She* was dating Solomon? Not to be judgmental, but she didn't seem like the kind of person an heir to an empire might date. No, Teddy had expected a debutante. Or a starlet. Certainly not a skinny, artsy looking girl with a welcoming sort of nonchalance to her.

"I'm not certain that's the best idea."

"Ah, don't worry about it. Mr. and Mrs. Miller aren't around n' only Solomon and Sterling are at the house. With both of them working, they're not very good company. Besides, I'm drowning in all the testosterone."

Teddy thought on it another moment. It really did seem bizarre, but there was something warm and familiar about the girl. "I suppose I am hungry."

The girl let out a happy sound and clapped. "Yay, alright then! Come with me. It's a bit of a ride, so I have one of the golf carts."

"Golf carts?"

"Yeah, come on. You'll see."

Teddy did indeed see as they walked around the garage because sure enough, there was indeed a golf cart there, painted a deep blue with mosquito netting pinned up at the sides.

"You really weren't kidding."

"No, why would I be?"

She didn't have an answer for that, so she just got in. The smaller, thinner girl hopped into the driver's seat and took off toward one of the worn paths that was too small for a car but plenty big enough for them.

It was surreal, but the real feeling of disbelief didn't quite hit until the huge manor loomed into view. Sure, she was aware that some of the richest people in the city would have a mansion, but it was even bigger than she had imagined.

Geez, it was like a sprawling city. The main part was practically the size of three houses and towered over the lawn with separate wings channeling out from either side of it and even behind it. She was sure it would take her at least an hour to walk all the way around the main property, and that was maybe if she jogged.

...or used a golf cart.

"It's something, ain't it?" Frenchie asked, chuckling lightly. Teddy could only nod, her words seeming to stick to the roof of her mouth. It was just so *big.* "I remember the first time I saw it. Nearly had a heart attack. Weird to think that there could be so much of us homeless folks while this one family is living in a place that could house 'bout a hundred."

Her words caught as something in Teddy's mind. "You're homeless?"

"Oh, uh, no. I mean, I was at the time. But now I'm... now I'm mostly not."

"...mostly not?"

She grinned and such a sappy expression crossed her face that was completely incongruous with the topic. "Yeah. I have a home, but someone bought it for me, so it seems... not real sometimes. But I have enough saved now to take care of everything when the bills start coming in, and I've done a lot to make sure it'll stay that way so... yeah. Mostly not homeless anymore."

"I see." Teddy wasn't quite sure she got it at all, but she

believed Frenchie. Frenchie was like her; she understood how the world worked and what it was to struggle. She knew what it was like to go to bed hungry and not know where the next meal was coming from.

"Anyway, come on in."

She pulled up to the side of the main part of the building, and then they were walking in what seemed to be a fancy side door. There was a small foyer, with coat hooks and a place to put muddy boots and galoshes, then they were walking into a *really* nice kitchen.

Most of it was all white and chrome, but there were a few hanging plants and other greenery that gave it lovely pops of color. Little splashes of life to make the space less sterile and more inviting.

But they weren't alone in the space. A figure stood up from where it was leaning on the counter and, sure enough, it was Solomon standing there.

"What are you doing out of your office?" Frenchie said, bounding over to him and pressing a kiss to his cheek. "Thought you'd be locked up in there until late."

"Decided to take a break. Was getting too upset about some peripherals."

"Anything you want to talk about?"

But he shook his head, his eyes flitting to Teddy. "No, that's alright. Was thinking of making some snacks."

"Well, great minds think alike because I was just gonna make me and Teddy here a light lunch. I noticed you've still got some fancy cheeses in there, so I was thinking cucumber and cream cheese tea sandwiches and the rest on the crackers I brought."

Solomon chuckled lightly, and Teddy took in the entire situation. The two of them interacted so naturally, with

Frenchie bouncing around happily and Solomon leaning toward her like a stalk of corn might lean toward the sun. It was clear that he thought the world of her, even just from the look in his eyes, and it was bizarre to see the quiet man who had hardly said a word during the contract negotiation be so relaxed.

"You know you don't have to keep bringing crackers as snacks. I'll make sure you're fed."

"Yeah, I'll stop bringing crackers when your mom stops buying those gluten-free, health-nut crackers. None of you have Celiac's or a wheat allergy, so she's just being fancy for the sake of being fancy."

Solomon huffed behind his hand, clearly trying not to laugh. "Her side of the family has a history of diabetes, and she loves her carbs."

"Yeah, yeah, that's what she tells y'all, but really she just buys them so her giant gorilla sons don't keep eating all her snacks."

"Oh, so we're gorillas now."

"Y'are if you got your mama resorting to buying those papery abominations just to make sure they don't get swiped."

"Alright, alright, fair enough. We're leaving Teddy out of the conversation."

"Oh, I don't mind," Teddy said, crossing over to perch on one of the stools around the island bar. "I am thoroughly entertained."

"Ah, thank God, another practical person around the house. I'm already in love," Frenchie said.

"Really?" Solomon questioned Frenchie. "It took me months to get that out of you, and the mechanic has that on the first day?"

In response Frenchie gave him a slap on the arm, and then

it was Teddy's turn to chuckle. After that, the conversation lulled as Frenchie went about making the snacks, with Solomon trying to help her only to be generally chased off every time he started to insert himself. It was cute and natural, and for the first time, Teddy found herself relaxing in the opulent place.

Of course, it helped that the snacks were all delicious. They really did have an assortment of 'fancy' cheeses, and the cucumbers were fresh and crisp. It wasn't exactly a filling lunch, but Teddy didn't want that, considering she was about to go back outside and work in the growing summer heat. Sure, there was air conditioning in the garage, but she couldn't use that if she was going to have the doors up, and she wanted to have the doors up to let the breeze and sunlight in.

They went through the snacks quickly, but before the last was gone, Frenchie was reaching over the counter to grip Solomon's hand. "Hey, before you lock yourself back up in the office, I made some treats for the chickies. You wanna help me feed 'em?"

The soft look that was exchanged between them almost made Teddy feel like she was invading. There was a raw sort of honest love between them, one she wasn't used to seeing. Her father had certainly never felt that way towards her mother, and Andre hadn't looked at anyone like that since she knew him.

"Yeah, that sounds nice."

"Alright, I'll be back in a minute to drive you to the garage, Teddy," Frenchie said happily, practically bouncing over to what must have been her worn backpack. "You can finish up the food. I see those muscles; you probably need the fuel."

And then she was gripping Solomon's hand and pulling him out of another back door, leaving Teddy alone.

Well, that was awkward.

The house was so big, so foreign, and without Frenchie and Solomon to fill it, it felt so cavernous. But that feeling quickly popped as the first door opened and none other than the twins were coming in, breathless with windswept hair.

"Oh." Silas was the first one to speak, looking startled to see her. "I didn't expect you to be here."

Yeah, the feeling was definitely mutual. Teddy blanched, hoping that it didn't seem like she was trying to shirk her work. Or worse, steal. "Frenchie invited me to come eat with her. So... I did."

"I see. Right. This is one of the days she usually visits. Where is she?"

Since when had they both grown so stilted? "She said something about feeding the chickies? Treats?"

"Okay, that makes sense. I think I'll go check on them."

He gave her a polite duck of the head and then followed the direction that the other two had gone off in. Some of the tension ebbed, but Teddy certainly wasn't relaxed to be alone with Sterling either.

"So," the younger twin said, sauntering over and grabbing one of the mini cucumber sandwiches, popping it into his mouth whole. "How's your first day going?"

"Alright. I wasn't exactly expecting the lunch on the house here though."

"Yeah, I bet." He chewed and swallowed, then snatched up a cracker, popping it into his mouth without any cheese. "So, what's a girl like you doing in a place like this?"

"Pardon?" she asked. It was pretty clear now, from his posture and the easy expression on his face that he was hitting on her. It was casual, so it didn't come across as creepy, really. But it wasn't something that she wanted, either. He was the twin of her boss, and not to mention part of an elite that she would never really understand.

"I get that you're a mechanic, which is definitely cool, but what I suppose I don't understand is why you're here. My family has guys, so why did my brother—who only really handles acquisitions—go all the way out to the city to hire another one? And, get this, after we talked, I checked into things, and I haven't found you added to the payroll at all. Even the freelancers we hire are on the database."

In addition to being handsome, the twins were both smart. Great. It definitely felt like God had stacked the deck when it came to the Millers.

"Hmm. That's strange."

But Sterling just laughed outright. For a moment she was afraid that he was about to reach out and touch her, but he grabbed his brother's glass and drained it before returning to a respectable distance away. Good, so he wasn't one of those pervs. Maybe he liked to flirt, but he seemed to know that there was a line and not to cross it.

"You're a cagey one, aren't you?" he asked.

"Again, I've been called worse."

He chuckled again, and the sound was so easy. "I bet you have."

"What do you mean by that?" Teddy asked, getting exasperated with the Miller brother who seemed intent on bothering her.

"Well ma'am, because you're a young, female mechanic and you've got enough scars on your knuckles to show you've been in at least a couple of fights. I'm sure plenty of people haven't liked that at all."

Great, so Sterling was observant too. Another thing to be wary of. As pretty as they were, as charming as they were, she only met any of these people because they were trying to buy out her home. Displace the people she loved.

"That's a mild way to put it," she said.

"Really? I don't think much of anything about you could be considered mild."

He was grinning at her again, all honeyed and charming as he stepped forward ever so slightly. And that was right about when Teddy figured him out.

At least a little bit.

It was sibling rivalry, plain and simple. Silas had brought her in, so she was technically 'his,' and Sterling was trying to insert himself into the situation. She remembered feeling something similar when Andre had first brought her in. Roman had been his *real* child and she was just an imposter. She remembered feeling jealous and defensive, and trying to be the saccharine, sweet daughter in a bid to earn Andre's favor.

But Andre didn't play favorites. He loved them equally, raised them as siblings, and it was through the months, and then the years of that kindness, that assurance that helped her move past it.

"You never know. I'm a multifaceted person," Teddy said.

"I don't doubt that. And what does it take to get to know these different facets of yours?"

She opened her mouth to shoot him down humorously, but then the door banged open and Silas was standing there, sun streaming in behind him.

"Hey," he said flatly to his twin. "Are you going to finish that proposal you were going to send to Dad?"

"Really? You just happened to come in because you were so pressed about that?" He stretched, pulling away from the counter. "I'll go do that now if it's such an issue."

"Thanks."

Silas' eyes then landed on her and, uh-oh, there was that awkwardness again. "I'm gonna go see if I can get Frenchie to take me back to the garage. This lunch is dragging on longer than it probably should have."

"Yeah. That sounds like a good idea."

12

———

Silas

He had messed up.

He had known that it was a bad idea from the beginning, and yet for some reason he had still done it, and now he was suffering the consequences.

Consequences that really mostly meant the mechanic woman was bothering him way more than he thought she would.

It wasn't even that she *did* anything, or at least anything that she wasn't supposed to do. For the most part, she tried to stay in the garage and fix or maintain whatever the other workers brought to her, but that still didn't stop her from popping into his thoughts all the time.

In fact, he couldn't seem to get his mind off her. And that fact wasn't helped since—for some reason—Frenchie seemed to have become super attached to the redhead in the three weeks since she'd started working on the ranch. So even though it was clear that Teddy was *trying* to stay out of the way, most Tuesdays she would have lunch in the manor.

A long lunch, too. At the insistence of Frenchie. Of course Solomon was so infatuated with his girl that he basically let her do anything she wanted. Silas tried to ignore her, to not go to the kitchen on Tuesday afternoons, but he still found himself running into her just as often as he didn't.

Silas grunted as he went into another set of reps on his bicep curls. He was about half an hour over his normal Thursday morning workout, but he was feeling pent-up, like too much energy was under his skin and he might burst at any moment. Thoughts were pinging around his head nonstop. He hoped that he could exhaust himself enough where they would give him a break for a minute.

But they didn't, and his thoughts went right back to Teddy. And *Sterling.*

His twin was weirdly into flirting with the mechanic every chance he got. Which normally wouldn't be *that* strange considering that Teddy was a gorgeous woman, but Sterling never showed interest in women for the most part. Like most of the Miller brothers, Sterling had a hard time trusting that a woman wanted to date him for reasons other than his money.

Sterling didn't trust *anyone*, let alone people outside of the family. He had watched his other rich friends get used, and even the ones that dated honest people often still ended up heartbroken. He wanted no part of it and had told Silas multiple times that he would marry some middle-aged church lady when he hit fifty just to shut Mom and Dad up.

Silas' arms were starting to quiver with all the weight he had been lifting, so he switched to a leg press. He should probably stop, but he didn't want to until his spinning thoughts did.

Everything was so *weird.* How Sterling was acting toward Teddy. How Frenchie was acting toward Teddy. Even how his own mind kept returning to her over and over again. Eventually, something had to give.

But after another half hour of working out, it was his muscles that waved surrender, not his thoughts. Heaving a sigh, he grabbed a towel from the shelf and draped it over his neck before heading out of his family's personal gym.

Technically, it was the secondary personal gym. His parents had one, but their equipment was different, most of it meant for rehabilitation and maintaining function. Dad had made it when Silas was quite young, and a freak accident with Mom had left her with three cracked vertebrae. She was alright, obviously, but it had been a long recovery, and the whole family wanted to make sure she had whatever she needed to stay mobile. And nearly twenty years later, the only thing she usually suffered from was stiff lower-back muscles and aches when it rained. They'd all been lucky that day.

Silas was so caught up in the memories, in recalling what it had been like to come home from school and hear that Mom had taken a bad fall, that he didn't quite realize where he was going until there was a sharp gasp from right in front of him.

But that brought him back *real* fast, and he blinked to find himself standing in the hall, Teddy just a few feet away from him.

Her green eyes were wide, and her face was shock-white. Her posture clearly conveyed how startled she was, far too startled considering the situation. It wasn't like he was *naked.* He was in a pair of gym shorts and a tank top. Sure, he was pretty sweaty, but—

Oh.

He was wearing a workout tank. Which meant his scar was

on full display, dark and red against the only slightly tanned skin of his chest.

Which meant she could see it.

"I-I-I was just trying to find the bathroom," she sputtered, reaching out to the doorknob beside her. Except that wasn't the bathroom either. It was a study. "Frenchie was on her phone and I didn't want to interrupt her, but I got kinda turned around."

Oh my goodness, she was staring at him like he was a monster. He knew the scar was an ugly thing, jagged and bubbled, but she didn't need to look at him like *that*. She was a mechanic and old enough where she'd had to have seen some gnarly things in her life... right?

But her gaze still roved over him, and finally he found his words again.

"Sorry about the scar," he grumbled, irritated that he had to apologize at all. This was why he always wore a polo or button-up. No one liked to look at that mess. It was gross.

She swallowed. "What scar?" she asked, almost sounding distracted.

Wait... what?

He didn't know what to say to that. It was right there in front of her, practically glowing like a beacon. Ugly and twisted. "Bathroom is back the way you came then to the left. Third door." And then he was turning and walking away. He could still feel her intense stare as he beat a hasty retreat, and he didn't stop until he was in his personal bathroom in his room.

He looked at the large mirror next to his shower. Yeah, his scar was still there, veined and hideous, reminding him how he had been so stupid as a kid. But the more he thought about the stunned expression that had been on Teddy's face, the less it seemed like she had been looking at him with revulsion.

No, it'd been something else written across her features entirely.

His heart thudded and he didn't know what to think about that, so he didn't think about it at all. Turning to the shower, he turned on the spray and told himself to forget all about her and the unfortunate run-in.

Easier said than done.

13

———

Theodora

Teddy reread the manual of the compact tractor she was working on for the third time, her eyes glazing over about halfway through the paragraph.

Again.

Grumbling to herself, she stood and took the lap around the inside of the garage, trying to clear her head. She was beginning to realize, as someone who had worked for her dad her entire life, she'd never had to worry about her employer being hot.

And boy, Silas was *hot.*

It was infuriating. She found herself distracted by him whenever he was around. That chiseled chin, the quiet sort of intelligence he had. The broad set of his shoulders. The way so many thoughts would flit behind those dark eyes of his. She wanted to know what he was thinking. She wanted to know *him.*

Teddy let out a growl of frustration as she paced. She wasn't some naïve maiden. She'd dated plenty of times from when she was sixteen until about three years ago, but it never really got that serious. She always had her mind on the shop and her future and family. Even some of the really nice guys she had dated ended up feeling like a second fiddle and broke things off.

Which was fine. She appreciated them knowing what they needed and knowing that she couldn't give that to them. And after that, she'd been pretty fine with not dating at all. Especially once the sharks started sniffing around the area. She had too much on her plate to consider dating, or even really being attracted to anyone.

And yet... she was *definitely* attracted to Silas.

Ugh, what a terrible cliché. He was rich and basically had an indentured servitude contract with her, and she was the one who had the idea for the whole deal in the first place. Having a crush on him was the absolute *worst* idea she could have.

It was all such a mess. How was she known for being put together when she was capable of making such a mess? None of it made sense.

Well, pacing wasn't doing her much good, so she returned to the manual and tried to read again. She was pretty sure she knew what she wanted to do on the mid-sized equipment, but she just wanted to be sure before she ruined something. It wasn't a super important machine; the workers had told her. But it was one they liked to use on smaller projects or repairing chunks of the fence. And the workers were nice, for as little time as she spent with them, so if they liked it, she wanted to fix it right for them.

"Hey, you there. What're you up to?"

Teddy was no longer startled by Frenchie's voice, but she did let out a small sigh. She'd been about to get her concentration back.

"Trying to work on this compact tractor," Teddy answered honestly. "Not doing so well. What're you doing here on a Saturday?"

"Solomon convinced his parents to go on this really nice cruise, so they're away from the manor for a couple weeks. Sal is at this power-lifting convention. The youngest brother is staying at college for a co-op opportunity this summer, and Samuel is still up with his aunt and uncle, so I'm spending a few days here. I wasn't sure if I'd find you, but since I did, I wanted to ask if you'd like to come see the horses with me."

"Horses?"

Frenchie nodded. "Yeah. I like 'em a lot. They're real sweet."

It was still before she would normally take her lunch and Teddy chewed her lip, wondering if she was taking advantage. "Should we maybe wait until my break?"

"Nonsense," Frenchie said with a laugh. "I asked Solomon first if it would be okay, and he said I could haul you wherever I wanted as long as I don't badger you. So if you wanna go, you can. But you don't have to, of course."

Teddy cracked a smile. "He really lets you do whatever you want, doesn't he?"

"Hardly," she scoffed. "But he has a real vested interest in me being happy, so he does maybe suggest that I goof around a bit more than I should. We're still finding a balance."

Frenchie held out her hand, and that was the first time Teddy noticed the thick callouses on the insides of her pointer and middle finger as well as spatters of color. Was Frenchie an artist? She'd never heard about it.

"So, ya wanna come?"

"I'm not gonna pass up horses. Sure, lead the way."

Frenchie did her jump-clap thing and then they were off, heading once more to her golf cart. It was actually a shorter ride to the stables, although it was out to the eastern side of things where she rarely went.

But of course, as they arrived at the stables, the sound of hooves came up from beside the building and then Silas was trotting into view.

Of course.

Of *freaking* course.

She couldn't just sit in the golf cart, so she got out after Frenchie and tried to act natural. Except it seemed like she had completely forgotten what acting natural entailed. Where was she supposed to put her hands? Was she breathing too hard? Blinking too much?

"Oh, hey there," he said, nodding to the two of them. "I was just finishing up. I'll be out of your hair soon."

"Don't worry about that," Frenchie said, waving her hand and opening the barn doors for him. "I'm just showing Teddy around. Neither of us is ready to ride around on our own."

He nodded and then he was going in, leaving Teddy to follow after. Gosh, her footfalls were so heavy. Why did she walk so loud? *Was* she walking loud?

She was staring down at her feet, so she didn't notice Silas getting down off his horse until she almost ran into his leg as it swung down. Thankfully, she caught herself and pulled up short.

"Sorry. I should have been more careful," Silas said as he landed.

Her mind immediately went to the last time she had seen him, all glistening from what had been either an intense workout or a full hour of him running for his life. She could feel the flush rising up her neck, which in turn only made her blush worse.

She felt like it might have been a bit rude the way she'd ogled him, but she'd been so surprised. He had been so *shiny*, and surprisingly ripped beneath the button-ups he normally wore. It was so unexpected, and then he'd said something about a mark or a scar—she hadn't really been listening—and then he was running away from her like she was a real creep.

Gosh, she was so lucky that she hadn't been fired.

"Oh, it's alright. I was distracted by..." *the image of your insane biceps and glistening clavicle* "...all the horses."

"They're a beautiful lot, aren't they?" he said with a smile. "They're all pretty sweet too."

"Yeah, they have to be, considering they're tolerating me," Frenchie said with a laugh, her hand in her pocket as she pressed kisses to the snoot of another horse.

"Frenchie," Silas said without looking, "you're not about to give Anabelle another sugar cube, are you?"

The girl stiffened, and the timing of it struck Teddy as particularly hilarious. "...why do you ask?"

"There are apples in the fridge. Go get one of those and cut it up for everyone."

"*Fine.* Spoilsport."

"You only think that because you're spoiled yourself."

"Yeah, yeah, keep raining on my parade and I'll go tattle to Solomon on you."

"Hey, let's not pit brother against brother," Teddy cut in, surprised at herself. But as the minutes passed, she was feeling less and less awkward. "We don't need a civil war."

"I dunno," Silas said with a wink. "Might be one anyway

between my uncle and dad any time now. Especially after Samuel."

"I've heard that name a couple of times now. Did something happen there?"

"It's a long story. Nothing you want to hear about now."

"But what if I do?" she challenged. She didn't know why she was feeling saucy, but she wasn't going to question it.

"Well, I guess it'll just have to remain a mystery." He finished getting all of his equipment off the horse and hanging it up, then went about brushing the pretty mount's coat. Teddy gave him a look, but he just continued on blithely.

"I guess you would need to rely on mystery if you have a boring personality," she said.

"Did you just call me boring?"

"I dunno. I guess it'll have to remain a mystery."

He laughed and it was such a nice sound. "I suppose I deserved that one."

"You said it, not me."

Frenchie came up behind them and grabbed her arm gently. "Come on, let's see some of my favorites."

Teddy almost wanted to protest, but she figured she couldn't without sounding strange, so she let the other woman pull her along.

Still, it wasn't so bad as Frenchie enthusiastically introduced her to several of the mighty steeds. Or mares. Teddy wasn't really sure on that part. She wasn't a horse girl.

But not too much time passed before Silas joined them, pressing more apple pieces into her hand. "Go on. They were fed this morning, so you're not spoiling their appetite or anything."

Maybe it was because of her crush, but the hand-off

seemed... significant, so she curled her fingers around the pieces carefully. "Thanks."

"Of course. No problem."

The time slipped by quickly, and before she knew it, all the apples were gone, and she'd met a good number of the horses. The mood was so lovely that they were all jolted when Frenchie's phone began to ring.

"Sorry about that," she said sheepishly before answering. The conversation was quick, and soon she was walking off, leaving Teddy and Silas alone.

And there came the awkwardness, rushing right back in like someone had left a window open. They stood there for a moment quietly, the only sound between them the not-so-soft sound of the horses munching on their apple pieces. Teddy knew she should say *something*, but by the time she opened her mouth, Frenchie was coming back.

"Hey, Solomon wants to go on a picnic, so he's gonna come pick me up. Silas, will you drive Teddy back to the garage and make sure the cart gets back to where it's supposed to go?"

Silas' eyebrows shot up, but he managed not to look horrified so that was good. "Sure, I can do that for you."

"Thanks, bro. I'll catch y'all later."

And just like that, Teddy was going to have to be alone with Silas for an extended period of time.

What was that about acting natural?

Her tongue was too heavy in her mouth and was she sweating? She felt like she was sweating. She was normally so poised and in control. She had to be to deal with some of the folks in her neighborhood. But it seemed the more time she spent with Silas, the more he affected her.

That couldn't be good.

They rode back the short way to the garage in relative

silence, with Silas pointing interesting things out every now and then and Teddy trying to answer like a normal human.

"Hey, I've been meaning to ask you something, but I'm afraid it'll come across as rude."

That broke her out of her canned answer and she swallowed harshly. Something personal? "Oh, what's that?"

"What's with the white streak in your hair. Is that like, some sort of comic book thing?"

Oh, whew. That wasn't that bad at all. "Are you telling me that you're familiar with comics?"

"Not particularly, but one of my cousins was super into them, so I always got a large dose from him every time we ended up seeing each other. And nice dodge of the question."

Ah, he'd caught her. "It's not a comic thing."

"Then what is it?"

"Why does it have to be anything?"

He seemed to think about that for a moment, and goodness did contemplative look real nice across his strong features. "I suppose it doesn't, but you're not the type of person who seems to do something for no reason."

"Huh, I think that's almost a compliment."

"Oh, it most definitely is."

They had reached the garage, but neither of them got out of the cart, just sat there, chatting.

"You don't have to tell me if you don't want to," he said finally. But she liked the curious look that he was giving her, like he was trying to puzzle her out. Maybe with anyone else it would have been invasive, but with him it was... it was...

Thrilling.

"I lost pigment in that part of my hair. But I like to hear all the reasons people tell themselves I've got a white streak at my temple," Teddy said.

"Lost your pigment? What, like an albino?"

She nodded.

"But, you've got your pigment everywhere else?" he asked.

Another nod.

"Is this like... a *really* specific form of vitiligo?"

Now *that* startled a laugh out of her. For some reason she hadn't expected him to know about that. "No, not vitiligo. It's poliosis."

He gave her a dubious look. "I never heard of polio giving someone white hair."

Another laugh. "It does sound like that, doesn't it? Nah, poliosis just means a chunk of hair loses its pigment. It can happen on any hair technically, but usually the scalp."

"Ah, and that's just... a random thing that can happen to people? At any time?"

He sounded curious, maybe a little concerned, but not mocking. He also sounded like he believed her, as much as he was asking questions. It was nice.

"It's not completely understood, but basically I had trauma to the side of my head when I was young—I pulled down a burning pot on myself. I was lucky that my mom had just emptied it of spaghetti, and it was sitting on the stove to cool. The burn wasn't bad enough for a skin graft, but they did have to transplant some follicles from the back of my head, and when those follicles started growing back, well something about the process must have traumatized them because all their melanin was *poof*."

"You're kidding! Just like that."

"Yup, just like that. The charity that helped me get the procedure was fit to be tied, but I don't know, I've always kinda liked it. It's like a battle scar, but a really pretty one."

A strange expression crossed his face. "I never thought of

scars as pretty." His tone was a bit weird too. Nothing bad per se, but definitely a shift from his curiosity moments before.

"I mean, maybe they're not in a conventional sense, but I like them. They tell stories. Kinda like roadmaps to past battles and lessons. And sure, sometimes they're a little intense, sometimes they can be awful, but they're a testament to survival. I admire that."

"And sometimes they're from someone doing something really boneheaded."

Well that was out of nowhere. "What?"

"Nothing." He shook his head, and then he was grinning at her. "So, now that I know your great hair mystery, do you have to kill me?"

"Nah, I owe you way too much money for that. I'd hate for your ghost to come and haunt me."

"Hah! And I would too. Just for something to do. I'm sure your life is thrilling."

"What gave you that impression? The white streak of hair or the fact that I saved you from a group of jerks with a baseball bat?"

"All of it."

Were they leaning closer to each other? It felt like it. And that didn't fill her with dread or fear. No, instead she felt excitement strike through her, building in her stomach and bubbling out to her limbs until—

"Hey, I was looking for the two of you," Sterling said, walking out of the garage. "Where'd ya go?"

"Frenchie took me out to see the horses but then had to run, so Silas offered me a ride back."

"I see. Sad I missed it." He stuck his hand in his pocket and took a stance that Teddy was *sure* he learned from some sort of old western where the main character came swaggering in.

"You know, I can always take you to see the horses at any time."

"Right. I'm sure you could." Whatever moment Silas and she had been having crumbled, and Teddy cleared her throat. "I better get back to work. I'll see y'all around."

"Is that an open invitation to visit?" Sterling asked with a wink.

She didn't miss how Silas stiffened beside her. "Uh, sure. Yeah. Whatever you want." With a wave to each of them, she rushed inside.

Geez. Messy, messy.

14

Silas

Silas knew that he should stay at the manor. That he should focus on some expense reports or go over Solomon's charity proposal or *something*, but instead he was driving his mom's bright pink golf cart to Teddy's garage for some repairs.

Not that it really *needed* repairs, but he wanted to hang out with the exact woman he should have absolutely no interest in.

Except he did.

He had a whole lot of interest.

He'd tried to keep a lid on it because it was pretty inappropriate, but seeing her with the horses had done him in. Her round cheeks had been so cute, along with the happy sort of laugh that escaped her mouth whenever one of the horses did something she liked. She was more honest and open with him than she had ever been, and for a moment it was easy to believe that the interest was mutual.

It wasn't, of course. It couldn't be. She was being polite, sure, but she clearly saw him as some sort of bloodthirsty shark at worst and her overly wealthy employer at best. Neither of those was grounds to cultivate anything more, so he was just throwing himself up against a wall by even caring.

But he wasn't used to wanting to cultivate anything at all, so sometimes it felt like he was twisting himself into knotted contradictions. Teddy had been working for them just under a month, barely a nick off of everything she would have to pay back. How was he supposed to not say something stupid for two or so more *years?*

He didn't really have a clue, but that lack of information didn't stop him from pulling into one of the open doors of her garage, beeping the horn.

"Oh my goodness gracious!" she said with a laugh, nearly doubling over. "Is this you're mom's ride? Please tell me you've brought me your mom's golf cart."

Her grin was so infectious that he knew he was returning it in kind. "In the flesh. Er... metal, rather."

"Man, Frenchie told me it was something, but geez, she really underplayed it."

"What are you talking about?" he joked, stepping out of the little vehicle. "I think it's demure."

"Oh yeah," she said with a nod between her peals of laughter. "Real understated."

That was about as long as Silas could hold it too, and soon they were both snickering. It wasn't that his mom's golf cart was ugly. It was just very... to a particular taste.

It was bright pink, with hazy lavender mosquito nets currently wrapped up and held in place with little mint bows.

The steering wheel was mint as well, with pretty pink roses embossed into the material. The top canopy was specifically 3-D printed to look like lace, with a durable plastic covering anything that would have been holes if it was made out of regular fabric. And that was pink too, of course.

The tires? Lilac. The seat covers? Mint with pink roses and vines. Even the hubs were a polished, pink chrome that caught the sun in iridescent waves.

"This is amazing," Teddy said, standing up straight. "You know that, right? Absolutely amazing."

He didn't mean for his gaze to sweep over her, taking in her broad smile and her wild hair and the slight flush to her cheeks. He also didn't mean to pause so much before he answered, but that was exactly what he did.

"Yeah, it is."

Maybe he said it wrong, or maybe he said it right, because her cheeks went even pinker and she shifted her gaze away from him.

"So, what are we doing today then?"

He wanted to say something witty, but that's not what happened. Why couldn't he be as smooth as Sal? Or maybe even Sterling. His brother seemed to have no problem flirting with Teddy every chance he got.

Not that Silas was jealous.

He wasn't.

...probably.

"Just a general workup. She hasn't been serviced in a couple years. Mom doesn't ride it around as much as Frenchie does. Or any of us really."

"But she uses it enough to totally trick it out."

"Well, Mom's got style. That's for certain."

"Too bad you didn't get any of that, huh?" Out of nowhere,

her arm playfully joshed his, and the touch should not have affected him as much as it did. But it was like her palm was fire, and he could still feel the press of her against his sleeve.

By some miracle, he was able to speak. "Are you trying to say I ain't got no style?"

"Well, not *no* style," she said and laughed. "But you're always so buttoned up and proper. I've only really seen you dressed down once. And that was when you were covered in sweat."

Oh. That meeting. The one that was burned into his mind. "I guess I just like looking professional. We can't all wear coveralls every day."

She let out a sound of mock offense. "Excuse you, these are *professional* jumpsuits, just so you know. And expensive too."

"Really? I may not be the best judge of things, but they don't exactly look high-end if you know what I mean."

"I'll have you know, finding plus size, female mechanic jumpsuits is quite the task. They're about three times as expensive than the male equivalent."

That didn't sound right to Silas. "Why not just buy the male ones?"

"Because even the plus-size male ones don't fit my hips and chest, and if I do get one big enough, the legs and sleeves are so long that they make me look like an Oompa Loompa playing in Wonka's closet."

Now *that* was a mental image. "Hah! Alright. Fair enough." He turned to her and they were almost face-to-face. He hadn't realized that she was so close. "For what it's worth, they look great."

"Uh-huh, you're just saying that so I don't mess up your mom's ride." She didn't step away from him, instead tilting her head upward to look him in the face. He hadn't realized that she had freckles. They were light, barely there, but there were a few under her eyes and across her nose.

"Nah, I trust you."

"Oh, you do?" she teased. "That's not something you hand around lightly."

"No, it's not," he answered, his throat tensing slightly. Since when was his saliva so thick? "But I already handed you a half mil, so I would have thought the trust was pretty implicit by now."

"You say that, but then we did have to sign a contract."

"That was for—"

"Both of our protection. I get it." She took a step away from him and he thought that was it, but then she was grabbing a water bottle from a mini-fridge and handed one to him. "Thirsty?"

"What?"

"You're licking your lips a lot. So, I figured you might be dehydrated."

"Ah, yes. Dehydrated. Yeah, probably." He took the bottle and gulped it down hastily, trying not to watch her throat as she did the same. How was she so pretty doing mundane things with her hair all wild and grease across her face? It didn't seem possible.

And yet it was, and he had to tear his gaze away from her yet again.

"Hey, you wanna make yourself useful?" she said once she was done.

"What do you need?"

She picked up a small toolbox and handed it to him. "Hold this for me while I go ahead and pop the hood."

"It's a golf cart, it doesn't have a hood."

She stuck her tongue out at him. "You know what I mean."

"No, I don't think I do."

"Do you want me to kick you outta my garage?"

"Technically it's *my* garage."

She put her hand on her hip and sent him a look that might have sent him running for the hills if he didn't know better. "Technically, it's your *daddy's* garage."

"Oof, that's below the belt."

She opened her mouth, plush lips curling at the corners, but quickly snapped it shut, her cheeks flushing again. Silas didn't think he had ever seen someone who blushed so adorably. "Just hold it, okay?"

Silas nodded and took it, wondering what she had been about to say. His mind shot out in about a dozen directions, and none of them he'd want his momma knowing about.

She crossed to the front of the golf cart and Silas followed her dutifully, holding the tool case. Teddy quickly grew serious as she got to work, opening up and looking things over.

"I need the flashlight," she said, holding out her hand.

Silas opened the toolbox, setting the thing on the ground and handing the flashlight to her. She took it, their fingers almost touching, and he wondered if there was something wrong with him for wishing that they had.

He had it bad.

But Teddy continued on blithely, completely unaware of what was going on in his head. It figured, the first time he had a crush since high school and it was with a woman who seemed to see him as some sort of predator.

And maybe he was. Or at least in a family of predators. Solomon's words echoed in his head, Pharisees and all.

"Alright, it's not too bad, but I definitely see some things I can flush. I think I wanna work on the brakes a little too, even if your mom's not exactly a speed demon."

She stood up and turned suddenly, bringing them face to face again. It was the second time in such a short amount of time that his heart still hadn't recovered from the first one.

"Oh. Hi," she said in a breathy voice, her pupils going wide as she stared up at him. "I didn't realize you were, uh, right there."

"Sorry," he said automatically, and he was glad that he had at least that response because his brain was certainly off-line. Gosh, he was twenty-eight. He was far too old to be so affected like some sort of giddy schoolboy.

"You..." she trailed off, swallowing, and there was that bob of her throat again. "You don't have to apologize. It's fine." Was she leaning toward him? It felt like she was leaning toward him.

Or was he leaning toward her?

He had no idea, and he never got his answer, because her phone let out a shrill ring.

They both jumped apart, and he felt like his heart was trying to climb all the way out of his throat.

"Sorry, I have to take this," Teddy said, reaching for her pocket in her jumpsuit. "If someone's calling me, it's almost always some sort of emergency."

"Yeah, I understand. Your family has a business."

She nodded and soon was walking away from him, her phone pressed to her ear. He turned away, as not to listen, and busied himself with scratching off some dirt from the side of his mom's cart just to have something to do.

It didn't seem like any time had really passed at all before Teddy let out a loud curse and a bang resounded through the space.

Whipping around, he saw her breathing hard, standing in front of one of the toolboxes, holding her hand.

"Whoa, you okay? What happened?" He crossed to her quickly, taking her hand in his. One of her knuckles was split, blood pumping up steadily, and it looked like another was already bruising terribly.

"I'm sorry," she said, trying to jerk away, but he kept a hold of her, pulling her toward where he remembered the first aid kit was. "This was impulsive. I'm not normally like this."

"Remember, you once saved my bacon by threatening people with a baseball bat."

She tried to laugh, but it came out more as a strangled sound than anything else.

"What's going on? Is everything alright?"

"No, none of it's alright." Her voice trembled and it made his chest hurt. She was always so strong, how scared or hurt must she be to be showing him any sort of crack in her armor? "That was my brother's public defender."

"He had bad news?"

She let out a bitter sound. "You could say that. They recused themselves and now he'll be appointed another one. That puts everything behind schedule, and the new lawyer will have less time to learn his case. That scumbag Cartwright is making things as hard as possible, and it just makes me so *angry*. I don't like being so helpless. It's not *like* me."

As she went on, her voice started to crack more and more, and he realized she was on the verge of crying, trembling a bit with the effort of holding it back. Once more, his mouth was moving before his brain did, anything to give her a lick of comfort, to let her know that she wasn't nearly as helpless or alone as she thought.

"I can cover a lawyer for you. My family has tons on retainer."

That seemed to shock her, and she stiffened, nearly pulling

her hand from his grip. But he just kept wiping away the blood with some cotton and then a sanitizer wipe, like his heart wasn't beating right outside of his chest.

"Why would you do that?"

He looked up for a moment, and her gaze was so intense that he looked right back down at her injury. He didn't have an answer for her.

Or he did, but he was afraid of what the true answer would be.

"It just seems to be the right thing to do," he answered finally, just before the pause grew excruciatingly long. If she had anything to say in response to that, she didn't, her posture relaxing slightly.

"I... thank you, Silas. I mean it."

Oh yeah. He definitely had it bad.

15

Theodora

It was hard to believe, but things were actually getting better. And although she still didn't quite get why, Silas had gotten them a bang-up lawyer who was apparently *thiiiis* close to getting Roman's case dismissed.

As if she needed a reason to like the guy even more. Her feelings were becoming a real menace to both her cheeks and her circulation, with her heart rate picking up every time she saw him and her face hurting from either smiling too much or way too many repeated blushes all in a row.

Ugh, she hated being so silly. It wasn't like anything would happen. Especially not considering how they had met. But she *had* meant what she said when she first met him. She just had no idea that he would end up being someone who saved her brother and their whole family business.

"Come on, Teddy. Concentrate."

She was under a big ol' truck in her dad's mechanic shop, almost everyone having gone home, but she was staying late to make up for some of the hours she had missed. Andre and Roman were starting to get a little suspicious of where she was flitting off too, but mostly she was able to cover it with her deliveries to the community and other gardening exploits. She wasn't sure how long that was going to last, but maybe she could think of a better cover story by then.

...probably not. Lately it seemed that all of her brainpower was dedicated to Silas and his charming smile and perfect hair.

Geez, everything would be so much easier if he was dumb instead of being so smart. But no, he was intelligent and funny on top of everything. Because life was unfair like that.

The buzzer sounded, pulling her from her thoughts, and she slid out from under the truck. It was her back door. When she thought about it, one of her little ones hadn't visited her in a while. She was overdue.

If anything could get her mind off of Silas, it was taking care of others, so she hurried over and let them in.

"Long time no see," she said, stepping to the side.

Sure enough, it was Antonio again, along with the much younger Manolito, although he always insisted that everyone call him Manny. They were both pretty scuffed up, with Manny's lip swelling already.

"Did you miss me?" Antonio said, although it was much more ragged than he probably meant it to be.

"Oh yeah, definitely. Now if only you would visit me when you aren't bleeding all over my doorstep." She clicked her tongue. "Come on in. Let me get the two of you cleaned up."

They obeyed, both seemingly too tired to even banter with her, and that was a pretty grim sign more than anything else. She cleaned Manny up first, Antonio knowing how to wash at the eye station and then the sink. As usual, it took quite a bit to get them even to the point where she could start bandaging things.

"You've got a pretty bad gash here," Teddy said when it was Antonio in front of her. "As usual, I recommend you go to urgent care to get this stitched and taken care of by a professional."

"You really think I got insurance, Mami? You know those centers don't take folks like us no more."

"Not without reporting us," Manny grumbled, one of the first things he'd said since he arrived. It was disheartening to hear a young one be so bitter, but it wasn't like she could blame him.

"Alright then, I'm going to glue this, but you need to make sure you take care of this, alright? You don't want a head wound getting infected. That's where your brain lives."

"Yeah, yeah. Just get it over with."

It wasn't the first time she'd glued together one of the kids, but she drew the line at stitches. She needed at least about a million certifications before she was willing to sew anybody up.

Antonio, to his credit, handled it like a champ, and after maybe an hour total, she was looking at two patched up young men.

"Alright," she said, taking a step back to look them over. "Do you two want some food, or do you wanna rush out?"

"Please, after all this? I need to eat before I fall over," Antonio said, trying for his normal smile. He almost got there but winced right at the end.

"Even if it's Roman's night?" Teddy asked.

"Even if it's Roman's night."

"Wow, alright then. Lucky for you, it was actually Andre's night. Come on."

The three of them headed up the stairs, although she took her time heading up. She'd never tell them, but she could tell that both of the young men were struggling to follow her, so she figured she could at least go slow.

Opening the door, she flicked on the light and strode forward, kicking off her shoes. The young boys knew well enough to follow suit, and then they were heading toward the kitchen, an eager look in their eyes.

"So he made some stroganoff—*ew*!" She had stepped into a puddle of cool water and it rushed up into her sock, making her whole foot wet. "Aw, come on, who spilled and didn't clean u—"

"Uh, Mami," Antonio said from just in front of her. "There's someone on the floor in here."

"What?"

She rushed around the corner, bile rising in her throat. She had no idea what he meant, no idea what he *could* mean, but then she was in the kitchen and she saw exactly what he was had meant.

Andre was there, laying in the middle of the kitchen, unconscious. A spilled cup and a broken plate were beside him, explaining the wetness, but the water didn't matter at all anymore.

"Dad!" she screeched, practically diving toward him. "Dad! I'm here. You'll be fine, I'm here now." She looked to the boys, who were staring down at her in shock. "Call 911! Please, quickly!"

Her voice was cracking, and her vision was starting to blur from tears, but she didn't pay them any mind. Her whole world was her father, laying sprawled out in front of her.

"No, no, *no, no, no!*" She hauled him into her lap, only a small amount of relief sparking in her when she noticed his chest rising and falling ever so shallowly. "You can't leave me, Daddy. Okay? You get that, right? You can't leave. I *need* you. Right here. *You can't leave!*"

He had to keep breathing. He *had* too. There was only so much that someone could ask her to survive.

She couldn't lose her only parent again.

16

─────────

Silas

He hadn't seen Teddy in a while.

He tried not to think about it because he wasn't completely pathetic, but after a few days, his mind kept returning to it again and again. She wasn't at the manor on Tuesday for her usual lunch. She didn't stop by the garage on her weekend day. If she was around at all, she had to be avoiding him, which was baffling because he was so sure that things were going well between them.

Something had shifted between them since that moment he had offered her a lawyer, holding her hand and cleaning her up like they were comrades instead of boss and employee. Sure, it was probably never going to progress anywhere beyond that, but that didn't matter. What mattered was that she seemed to be trusting him. That she was letting him in.

Was he wrong entirely?

He couldn't quite say. He'd been busy himself. Half of the time he felt like he was trying to dodge his dad, fearing the man would order him to do more acquisition investigations of Teddy's neighborhood. But he also was trying to work more on the ranch, trying to learn more of how things worked. He was beginning to feel like all their automation had stolen a lot of the love he had of the field. And also... maybe added more cruelty than there needed to be in the process.

They were separating mothers from calves on a regular basis, and he couldn't help but see the sorrow in those animals' eyes when they looked around for their young ones. He also read that cows had best friends, but they weren't really given much time to roam around, so they didn't get to play together very often.

He knew that animals were put on earth by God and man as their guardians, but there was a line. They deserved respect and honor. Was his family doing that? He was beginning to think they weren't. Were his uncle and aunt out west onto something?

Silas shook his head, trying to pull himself off his own tangent. Right, it was Tuesday again and there was still no lunch at the manor, so he was searching for Frenchie.

He found her outside, sunbathing as she drew in her sketchbook. He almost felt bad interrupting her, considering she looked so content while she bobbed her head to her music, but he was beginning to get worried.

"Hey," he said, walking around to stand in front of her. She took her earbuds out and shot him an easy grin. "Do you know what's up with Teddy? I haven't seen her in a while?"

Frenchie's mouth fell open slightly and the look on her face wasn't a good one. "*Oh.* You haven't heard?"

That was not a phrase that anyone ever wanted to hear. It was never uttered before good news. Never.

"Obviously not, considering I'm asking you now."

"Oh, right. Of course, sorry. Her father had a stroke and has been in the hospital. She called like... sometime last week? Solomon said she could take as much time off as she needed and not to worry about anything. Family first and all that, ya know." Her serious expression grew a bit softer. "Do you think he would have done that before?"

But Silas was just standing there. He knew the words that she had spoken were English, but they didn't make any sense.

Father?

Stroke!?

"Done what before?" he rasped, feeling like his mind was a hamster that had been knocked completely off its wheel and was now scrambling to get back on. Hundreds of thoughts barreled through his mind. Was she alright? Was her father alright? What hospital were they at? Was he getting the proper care? Was he back at home?

"Would he have given her all that time off? It's probably crazy, but I feel like, sometimes, maybe we've both changed for the better," Frenchie said.

He only just realized that Frenchie was trying to have a conversation with him, and he yanked himself back to the present. "Um, yeah. I can't say about you, but yeah, there's been some changes in Solomon lately."

"For the better?"

"That part's hard to say, but they seem positive so far."

She nodded, seemingly comforted, and that seemed to be the end of the conversation.

Except it didn't *feel* like the end of the conversation. Silas was still left blinking in shock, his thoughts still going a million miles an hour.

Teddy hadn't contacted *him* at all, and technically the contract was between the both of them, not Solomon.

Then again, why would she? They weren't particularly close, and it wasn't like he knew much about her beyond the fact that she had poliosis. He certainly hadn't shared much about himself, for all the joking they did together.

Footsteps sounded and then Sterling was beside him. "Hey twin, where'd that big girl go?"

"What are you on about?" Silas snapped; his tone much harsher than he would normally use on his brother. "Why are you talking about anyone that way?"

"Whoa? What's wrong with you? Big isn't an insult, you know. And it's not like she's not hot. If she wasn't covered in grease most of the time, she'd probably have a fan club to rival Solomon's."

"*Sterling,*" Silas heard himself hiss. He didn't like his twin talking about her so casually. Even if he was right. She was plus-sized, and she was gorgeous, but when those words tumbled from his brother's mouth, they didn't seem *respectful.* "Her father is in the hospital. She hasn't been around because he had a *stroke.* A little respect would do you well."

"Hey, alright. I'm sorry, I'm sorry. I didn't realize your girl-friend was in a bad spot. How about a little mercy for your brother... "

"*Respect*, Sterling. *Respect.*"

He held up both of his hands. "Geez, calm thyself. I'll try talking to you when you've calmed down." He rolled his eyes and headed off.

For once, Silas wanted to take his brother and rattle him until he stopped being such a jerk.

Silas took a deep breath, looking to where Frenchie had been but realizing that she had packed up and headed off during his and his twin's argument. He had a feeling that they might have chased her off, and that made him feel guilty.

It also made him realize that he wanted to do something for her.

Teddy that was, not Frenchie. Although maybe he should get her a thank-you gift for tipping him off.

But one thing was certain, he had to do *something.*

IT WAS about an hour and forty minutes before he was pulling up to the mechanic shop, which was closed, of course. He wasn't surprised, considering that Teddy's father was in the hospital. If he was in the same situation, he wouldn't be up for oil changes and inspections.

Putting his car into park, he went to the front and knocked, wondering if maybe some workers were around.

Nope. No answer. It seemed that the whole place must have taken off. Silas wondered if he should call her, but he kind of wanted to surprise her, maybe make her smile a bit more than "Hey, I'm outside your job. Answer please."

Then again, maybe she was working on some cars to help her calm down, little side projects. He'd noticed that she always liked to have something to do with her hands, so that made sense. He could always go check out back and see if she was there, and if she wasn't, then he would figure out where to go from there.

He headed around the building, hands in his pocket, hoping that he didn't look sketchy, but when he reached the rear, he saw that he wasn't the only person waiting there.

Clearing his throat, he watched as the three younger people jumped, clearly surprised by him.

"What the hell are you doing here?" the tallest of the trio asked. He looked like he had gotten out of a fight a few days earlier, some bruises almost faded from around his nose and what had definitely been a very deep cut glued together on his forehead.

"I'm here to see Teddy," he answered calmly. Although the last time he had been in the alley had been dangerous, he was pretty certain the teens in front of him weren't looking for trouble. "What are you doing here?"

"We're looking for Teddy," the smallest answered, a young girl who looked like maybe she was thinner than she was supposed to be but wasn't nearly as banged up as the first speaker. "She usually patches us up, but she ain't been around much. We were worried about her."

"Yeah," it was the largest and oldest one speaking again. "Last I was with her, it was real bad and they rushed her and her dad to the hospital. I've been checking in every day, but she ain't come back yet. I would call her, but I ain't got a celly and I never memorized her number. She was always just here, ya know?"

Of course, Teddy had a rag-tag group of children that looked to her for healing and protection. She was exactly the type of person to put herself out there like that.

So much for his surprise. "I was hoping she might be around here," Silas admitted. "But I can call her for y'all."

All three of them brightened. "Really? You would, man?" the biggest one asked.

"Yeah. Just gimme a moment."

Pulling out his phone, he gave one last mental goodbye to

the grand gesture that he wasn't going to finish cooking up and dialed Teddy's number. He'd saved it, of course, after that first day that she had contacted him. And since then, he'd spent many minutes debating on texting her about something funny or superfluous before always deciding not to in the end.

She picked up on the second ring, sounding drowsy.

"Hey, Silas. Did Solomon not tell you that I'm off?"

Oh geez. Was she getting enough sleep? Was she sleeping in the hospital? That couldn't be comfortable, no matter how devoted she was to her dad.

"He did. I'm actually calling because I'm outside of your shop—"

"Why are you outside the shop?"

"—and there are a few kids here waiting for you. They said they were worried because last they saw; you were piling into an ambulance. Is everything okay?"

She let out a long sigh, and then there was some muffled background noise. He guessed that she was probably walking out of her father's room into the hall, judging by the uptick in volume.

"Everything's fine for what it is. You can tell them that." She hesitated again, but Silas could tell there was something else she wanted to say. "Can you... do me a favor?"

"Of course. Anything you need." Maybe he agreed too readily to it, but he was mostly past the point of caring. He wanted to *do* something.

"Could you ask them if they've eaten?"

They probably shouldn't have, but the corners of his lips ticked upward. Naturally, she was worried about that. When he'd first met Teddy, he thought she was cold and abrasive, but clearly that was just a front.

"Hey, kids, you hungry?"

"We ain't kids," the tallest objected. "I'm *seventeen*."

"Alright," Silas shot back. "But are you hungry?"

The trio exchanged a look and that was all he needed. "Yeah, they look pretty ravenous."

"Okay, I'm going to give you the code to the garage. Let them in and get them some of the leftovers we have in the fridge. They're about to go bad anyway. There isn't much, but it'll be enough to hold them over until I get there in an hour or two."

"Oh, you don't have to come all this way if you don't—"

"No, it's fine. I need a change of clothes and some other things. Plus, the stuff in the fridge needs to be used by someone, and I'd rather it be some hungry kids than the trash can. I'll see you in a bit. Look for my text; it'll have the code."

And then she hung up, leaving him with three uncertain gazes sizing him up.

"She said she's got some food up there to take the edge off and she'll be by to cook in a bit. Let's all go in, shall we?"

They gave various affirmative answers and then they were moving. The text came just as Teddy had said, but once they were inside, Silas had no idea where to go.

"This way," the tall one said, leading him through the space and over to a staircase that he hadn't even noticed. "The apartment's up here."

"Thanks," Silas said, closing the garage door and making sure it was locked before bringing up the rear of their little formation. "You know your way around pretty well."

"Yeah, and you don't, so I'm guessing you ain't her boyfriend."

There was something defensive about the way he said it,

and Silas couldn't help but wonder if maybe the boy had a little teenage crush. "No, not her boyfriend. Just a friend."

"I dunno why Teddy never has a boyfriend," the smallest said. In reality, she probably wasn't that much younger than the other two, but she was definitely quite petite, her features pointed, almost elfin, with full lips and a dark, thick, curly bun atop her head. "She's so pretty and strong."

"Teddy knows there ain't no one around here worth her time," the middle one spoke up, the first time he'd chosen to do so since Silas had arrived. "She deserves like, I dunno, a football player, or like... a college teacher or something. Someone real cool and smart."

The largest one opened the door as Silas tried to hide his grin. Although it was strange, it was nice to hear the young ones admire Teddy so openly. Made him feel a little less silly about doing it himself.

"Her boyfriend is her toolbox," he said as Silas crossed over the threshold. "Because that's all Teddy needs. Ain't a man alive that can compare, and she knows it."

"Not even you, Antonio?" the youngest asked precociously.

"Not even me."

He gave a *very* pointed look to Silas, which the Miller brother tried very hard not to grin at. Which was quite a challenge, considering how earnestly the young man was posturing. Maybe it should have been annoying, but it was cute more than anything else. It was clear the young man valued Teddy very much.

"How about those leftovers?" Silas said.

The mention of food had all of the young ones hurrying to the table in the kitchen. Although Silas didn't say anything, he was surprised by how *small* the place was. Teddy, her father and her brother all lived in the same space? That didn't seem possible. Was he that out of touch with things?

He didn't ask that out loud, however, and focused on feeding the children. They wolfed everything down as quickly as he could microwave it, then looked to him for more.

"You're gonna have to wait for her to show up for that," Silas said with a laugh. "She didn't give me permission to use all her things, so I'm not going to."

"That's alright. I bet you can't cook without the help anyways," the tall one said. It might have been meant as a joke, but it did poke at Silas' pride. "We should clean up. Teddy'll probably be upset if she comes back and things are messy."

"She normally pretty neat?"

"Nah, not really. But her dad is, and they all keep the place nice for him."

"Right. Well I can get behind some cleaning. Do you all know where the supplies are?"

"It ain't that big a place. We'll find them."

That logic made sense to Silas. They spread out, and sure enough, some of the cleaning supplies were underneath the kitchen sink, some were in a small closet in the bathroom, and the rest was tucked into a tall, skinny cabinet in the very corner of the kitchen.

There wasn't a ton to clean, but there was a small layer of dust in certain areas, and the floor definitely needed to be swept. It looked like someone had dropped a plate of food or something, and instead of cleaning it up, the bits of nutrition had been kicked around. It wasn't until he went to take out the trash and saw both a broken cup and plate that he began to realize maybe that scattered food had more of a reason than he had previously thought.

But he quickly dismissed that and continued to work.

Teddy ended up taking longer than she said she would, and it was getting to be well in the afternoon when he heard a rattling car pull into the back of the garage.

"I think I hear her," the tallest said from the bathroom. The young man had demanded to clean it all on his own, and now Silas was sure that the kid had a crush on Teddy and was trying to impress her.

Again, it came across as much sweeter than it probably should have.

Speaking of crushes, Silas didn't want to look flushed and mussed when she came up the stairs, so he hurriedly splashed water onto his face and patted himself dry with a rough paper towel and tried to fix his hair in the faint reflection on the window behind the kitchen sink. It would have to do.

He turned around just as she came in through the door, and she looked around uncertainly. And goodness, she looked *rough.*

Silas felt concern bloom in his chest, accompanied by worry and a softer, fizzier something that he didn't want to name. Her hair was wild and clumped in different spots, like she'd been tossing and turning all night, unable to find a comfortable position. The skin on her face was reddened, probably dried out by the hospital air, and there were *dark* circles under her eyes. If he didn't know better, he would almost think they were bruises, they stood out so starkly against her alabaster skin.

"Hey, it smells nice in here," she murmured, trying to crack an appreciative smile. But the expression came out as more of a grimace, her lips dry and pale. "Like lemons."

"We've been cleaning!" the tallest of the trio said, practically barreling down the hall. "Wanted to make things nice for you when you got home."

"Aw, that's sweet of you guys." She took off her shoes and then opened her arms wide. Silas watched as all three went to her at once, latching onto her with tight hugs like she was a bastion in the storm.

He supposed for them, she was. What had they said? That she patched them up? So when they were hurt, bleeding and scared, she was the one they went to. How terrified they must have been when they didn't know where she was or how she was. He was glad that he had been able to connect them all again, if only for the sheer relief that was so evidently pouring out into the room from them.

She made their world better. She made the *actual* world better. And when he slowed down to think about it, could anybody say the same of him?

That thought coiled sourly in his belly and licked up his spine to whisper in his ear. Of course, his family loved him and would be devastated. But if he were to disappear tomorrow, would the world be any worse off? Would anything be lost?

Sure, his dad would have to find a new man to specialize in speculative acquisition, and Silas' horse sure would need another rider. Sterling might get worse, act out more. But that was it. For all his power, for all his money, he was suddenly realizing that he didn't really amount to...

...well, *anything.*

It was a sobering thought and he had to force himself to shove it to the back of his mind. He was supposed to be helping Teddy now, not bemoaning his sudden rush of inadequacy.

"Glad to see you home."

"Still not sure how you ended up here, but it's nice to see someone not in scrubs. I'm gonna go clean up, and then I'll get started on the food."

"Uh..." the tallest murmured, pulling away from her slightly. "I wasn't totally done cleaning the bathroom. Can I have like, I dunno, ten more minutes?"

Her red eyebrows went nearly up to her hairline. "You, Antonio, who can't even be bothered to tie his shoelaces right, cleaned my bathroom of your own volition?"

The young man's tanned skinned quickly flushed, going all the way down to his oversized shirt collar. "Ay, well, you know how it is, Mami. I just wanted to help out."

Teddy let out a soft, very tired laugh and pressed a kiss to his forehead. "Thank you. You're amazing. You finish up cleaning the bathroom, and I'll put the rice cooker on and get everything set out. That should give you plenty of time."

"Alright." He gave her one last squeeze and rushed off.

"Can I help you in the kitchen?" the middle one asked, reminding Silas that he was indeed capable of speaking. "I wanna learn."

"Of course. Let's all go wash our hands then. Silas, why don't you sit down for a bit?"

He wanted to interject, to say that he could do something else, but instead he nodded and found a seat that was out of the way at the kitchen table. He got the feeling that maybe Teddy needed the simplicity of one thing at a time, so if she wanted him to wait while she taught the younger ones kitchen things, then he was more than happy to.

Which turned out to be quite a good decision—because watching her interact with them was like learning about an entirely different side of her, a secret one. One that only a select few were privy too. Despite how obviously weary she was, she was never rough or impatient with the young ones. She never sighed in irritation at their questions, slang or memes that Silas most definitely didn't understand. Instead she laughed with them, encouraged them, taught them gently and patiently.

It was beautiful. It was tender. It was Teddy without all of those walls and protections that she had up to defend herself from the unfairness of the world, and goodness if it didn't make his heart *ache* in the best possible way that she was trusting him with that.

"Hey, Mami, I'm done in here if you wanna wash up."

She looked up from where she had been showing the youngest how to cut properly and protect her hand, relief palpable across her features.

"Thanks, Antonio. I'll be there in a moment." Her eyes flicked to Silas. "You mind chaperoning this? I really need to wash up."

He was on his feet before he even realized his brain had given the order. "Of course. I don't mind."

More relief. He found that he liked that expression very much on her and wished he could lighten her burdens all of the time. Sometimes he felt like she was so stressed and tightly wound that she might randomly combust in front of him someday. "Alright, I want you two to *very* carefully finish cutting this avocado, and then the peppers. If you still have time, you can try dicing the cilantro and adding it to the rice. I should be out by then."

"Don't worry," the middle one said matter-of-factly, not missing a step with his chopping. "We got you."

Another kiss, this time pressed to the top of his head. Silas had never seen Teddy so open with her affections. Would he ever be able to earn that kind of tenderness? That closeness? Probably not, and it wouldn't do to be jealous of impoverished children, so he needed to move his brain right along.

"Yeah, I'm sure you do, Kayden," she said with so much

warmth that Silas' heart almost melted right then and there, then she was padding off to the bathroom.

"Alright," he said, stepping up to the counter with the two young teens—pre-teens? He actually had no idea how old any of them were besides Antonio. They were dutifully working on the fare. "Let's go nice and slow. I'm not exactly an expert at this myself."

"You don't know how to cook?" the youngest girl asked as if that was the craziest thing that she'd ever heard.

"I know how to cook," he answered with mock offense. "... like four different dishes," he finished with a wink.

Good, that got a giggle out of her. He was getting the feeling that they were warming up to him, even though he clearly was someone who wasn't one of their own. Who knew, if he could win them over, maybe he could eventually get to Teddy's inner circle.

Or maybe it was best not to think about things like that.

Teddy ended up spending a good, long time in the shower and dinner wasn't exactly a quick affair, so it ended up being quite late by the time Silas was standing at the kitchen sink, washing dishes and looking out at the night sky. Blue velvet sinking into waves of indigo velvet followed by the deepest of eggplants before, eventually, it turned that specific shade of pitch black that only the city could get.

The manual task soothed him, smothering the embarrassment that he had naively asked where their dishwasher was when the meal was up. He was doing something with his hands. He was being productive.

He was making a difference. Even if it was a small one, it

was *something*, and it was for someone who so clearly deserved it.

"Oh man, when did it get so late?" Teddy asked, looking out of the window beside him.

"It's been late," Antonio said, yawning and rubbing his stomach. The kid certainly had packed a lot away. It would have been impressive if it wasn't also a little sad. "We'll get out of your hair."

"No," Teddy said quickly before clearing her throat. "No. I don't want y'all wandering out tonight unless you're expected. Why don't you two boys sleep in Roman's room and Jamani can take my room. Then y'all can eat breakfast in the morning and clear out."

Even Antonio looked surprised by that. "Are you sure, Mami? It ain't no big deal, going out at dark. You know that."

"Yeah, yeah, you're big and tough. Let's just say I'm feeling tender and protective lately, so humor an old woman. Unless you've got a curfew, I'd much prefer you stay here."

There was concern and sadness when the three of them all confirmed there was no one waiting for them. No one who would miss them. If Silas was staying out overnight, he usually at least texted his twin to let him know he was alright. These kids really had nobody?

It wasn't hard for Teddy to get them all to agree to stay after that, then it was some gentle corralling to the bathroom in a staggered order to get them to wash up, and then into the appropriate beds. By the time all of that was done, Silas had washed all the dishes, dried them too and then put them away.

"They're good kids," she sighed wearily when she finally joined him again.

"I don't doubt that," Silas said cautiously. "But where are

their families? Why don't they have someone who cares where they are?"

She gave him a weary sort of shrug. "You wouldn't get it."

It stung, but he knew why she said it. With as earnest a tone he could manage, he reached out to place a hand on her shoulder. "I could try, if you would explain it to me."

Another one of those long sighs. But instead of turning away from his touch, she stepped into it, turning so that his arm was across her shoulders. It wasn't quite a hug, but it was a supportive thing. Something someone might do with another someone if they trusted them. If they were looking for comfort.

"Antonio has a good family, but there's seven kids there. He's old enough that he's expected to take care of himself, and honestly, when he's gone, that's one less mouth to feed."

"Seven kids? That's more than my mom. His must have been very busy for a hot streak there."

She shook her head. "I'm not actually sure it's his mom. I don't even know if his mother's in the country. I think it's his *tia.* As for Kayden, he does live with his mom, but she's a nurse full-time. At first, she spent *so* much money on babysitting, trying to do right for him, but eventually we stepped in and told her we would handle it."

"We?"

"Yeah, we. You know, the community. It was Mrs. West's idea first, actually, but it spread pretty quickly. So now there's a network of about ten of us who are trusted by a couple of the parents around here who will watch and feed him for free."

"And Jamani?"

"I think she's one of the street kids from the eastern part of the city."

That surprised him. "You *think*? You mean you don't know if she's running around out there with no family?"

"No. I do think she has a family. That's how she stays protected. But at the time she was born, her mother was underage and her parents were pressuring her into giving up her baby against her will because they didn't like the skin color of the father. You didn't hear that from me, of course."

Silas digested that for a minute. "You know her mom?"

She shook her head. "No. Not really. But I may have had a part in... ferrying someone to where they would be safe when I was too young to even have a license. Perks of having a big ol' service van at the time."

"And so now her daughter visits you?"

"From time to time. I'm sure her mother wishes she wouldn't, but she's fourteen, you know, and she, therefore, knows everything."

Silas chuckled at that. "I remember the age. It was nice— for a year or so—to understand the entire world."

"Boy wasn't it." She leaned back a little, her soft form pressing into his arm. "So yeah. It's not like I'm some bastion of goodness in this town. If I wasn't here, there would be other warm hands and hugs waiting for them. I don't want you to think I'm some sort of savior of this community and everyone else is some heartless jerk."

"I didn't think that at all."

"Good. Because I'm aware of what this looks like, and it's not that. I don't think I'm coming here like some missionary to save the poor people. These *are* my people, and I'm just trying to pay back everything they've done for me."

Silas nodded. He hadn't been thinking that in the slightest, but he understood why she felt the need to tell him. He had figured out that maybe Teddy wasn't Andre's blood child. He was also aware that his family would probably make some strange assumptions if they ever saw her with her brother or father. He was also aware of how someone like Teddy, who was so fiercely protective of those she loved, would try to head all of that off whenever she could.

"They like you, though. I hope you can tell that," he said.

The smile on her face was so sweet that he wanted to frame it. Remember it forever. "They like that I patch them up and don't tattle on them."

"I think that's simplifying it."

"Maybe." She turned so that she was looking up at him, her front pressed into his side. He turned in kind, and they were just a breath away from each other again. He swore he could hear her heart beating through the scant bit of air between them, a demanding counter rhythm to his own.

"I should go. It's my turn to stay overnight at the hospital, and Roman's going to be coming home to sleep on the couch."

Her breath was warm and smelled slightly of the food that they had made. Spicy, welcoming. It tickled along the bottom of his chin and curled slightly over his face. He wondered what it would taste like if he—

"I can drive you to the hospital if you need," he said, trying to rein himself in. Teddy was being close to him, trusting him, because she was exhausted and in need of a haven. Taking advantage of that would be reprehensible.

Even if she did look like she had the most kissable lips.

"Nah, I've got things handled. I gotta get the junker back so Roman can take it home."

"Right, right. That makes sense."

"I...I really should go..."

Although she said that, it seemed like she was leaning again, her head turned up to his. It would be so easy, *so* easy, to tilt his own downward and press their lips together.

They were sure to be soft; he knew that. They were no

longer dried from the hospital and her chewing on them, seemingly refreshed by the shower and whatever her beauty regimen was. They would be warm, like her.

He really needed to think about something else.

Clearing his throat, he took a step back. "Well, I best be on my way then."

She blinked a moment, as if she was surprised that he had moved. "Uh. Yes. So I can leave. That would be smart."

"I've been known to be smart from occasion to occasion."

"I'll remind myself not to get used to it then."

There, back to their usual banter. He hadn't ruined anything in his moment of weakness. She didn't know how badly twisted up inside he was about her.

But as he walked to the door, about to show himself out, he couldn't help the question that arose in his mind then barreled its way right out of his mouth.

"Teddy?"

"Yeah?"

"Are you gonna be alright?"

That time her smile was wan as she answered, speaking of so many other losses and scares. "I'll manage. I always have."

"You know you're not alone in this, right?" Silas said.

There, that made her smile ease a little, some of the darkness at the edges flee. "Yeah. I ain't been alone ever since Andre took me in, and I try hard never to forget that."

"Good. That's good." He wanted to tell her that it wasn't just Andre or her family. That she had *him* too. But it wasn't the time. It probably wouldn't ever be the time.

So with one last nod, he shut the door and guided himself down the stairs. But as he headed around the front to get to his car, he realized that he wasn't satisfied.

He wanted to do more.

Goodness knew that she deserved it.

But what was he supposed to do for the woman who insisted on taking care of everyone around her and never really taking the time for herself? That was a challenge, alright. But one he was up for. He was going to make a difference. Even if it was for just one person, no one would be able to say that he hadn't brought some light into the world.

Because even a singular light could chase away so much of the darkness.

17

Silas

He showed up the next day, bright and early. He knew Roman was going to be home, and he wanted to catch the man before he left to do anything the family might have needed to get done.

It took several rounds of knocking, however, to get Roman to answer, and when he did, he instantly looked suspicious.

Silas didn't entirely blame him for that. They'd only met once, the day Silas and Teddy had struck their whole arrangement, and the rancher got the feeling he had no idea about any of the financial details of that transaction.

"Can I help you?" he said cautiously. His voice was a low rumble, much lower than Teddy's, but Silas could pick out the same kind of cadence to their way of talking. He'd put money down that they must have both picked it up from their father. "We're closed, so we're not doing any work right now."

"Oh, I know," Silas answered quickly. "That's why I'm here."

"I don't follow."

"I heard about what happened with your family, and I kind of wanted to do something nice for your sister. Frenchie —that's my brother's girlfriend—just adores her. And Teddy has been a huge help back at the ranch, so I was wondering if you could point me in the direction of something I could do that would really take a load off her. Something *important*."

The man's dark eyes narrowed as he regarded him, as if he really was trying to puzzle out if Silas was genuine or not, before slowly nodding. "I think she mentioned you once or twice. Apparently, you guys aren't as bad as we thought."

Huh, that was good to know. "Well, you know, we try not to be monsters. Except on the full moon."

He didn't laugh. "Well come in. She told me that the kids cleaned the place yesterday, but I'm sure there's something we can find." He stepped back to allow Silas in. "I'm sure you've noticed, but my sister can be kinda..."

"Independent?"

"Yeah, I guess that's right. She doesn't like relying on anybody or feeling like a burden, so it might be hard to find much."

That made Silas' stomach sink. If her own *brother* couldn't think of something great to surprise her with, to help her with, then what chance did he have?

"Maybe something down in the shop? I know I'm no mechanic, but I can clean well enough. Organize maybe? Polish a hood?"

"Oh no, never touch how she has her tools organized. She'll flip. Made that mistake once when she was first learning, and she chewed me out for what felt like two weeks. Apparently..."

he smirked ever so slightly before continuing, "we keep the ones she likes too high to reach."

It was so easy to picture that exact scene. While Teddy was not anything near short, her brother was over six foot and a couple inches taller than Silas himself—and that wasn't counting his impressive hair. He was sure that hopping up and down or having to find a footstool to grab what she wanted had been the most adorable sight.

"Alright. So, the apartment's been taken care of. The shop is out for the most part. Surely there's gotta be something?"

Roman looked around, rubbing his chin. "Yeah, I know there's something, but I kinda just woke up, so it's like I'm trying to think of all the things she does on her own. Like... you know, maybe you can do something nice to her bike she does deliveries with. *That's it!*" Suddenly his face broke into a huge grin and he clapped his large hands. "Her garden!"

Silas blinked at him. "Her what?" He'd been around the place plenty and hadn't seen anything even remotely resembling a garden.

"Come on, let me show you."

The big man moved surprisingly fast, turning on his heel and heading toward a door that Silas had never noticed before. It wasn't in the garage part of the building, but rather the reception area, and there wasn't an exit sign on it. He supposed his mind had dismissed it as a potential storage closet. Or unmarked bathroom.

But it wasn't either of those things, and soon they were stepping outside into such a dense gathering of green that he almost wondered if he had been somehow teleported back to his mom's garden.

"Wow!"

Looking around, he realized he had spotted it once before,

the fence that is. A tall, brown privacy fence was erected around it, hiding all the beauty inside. Everything was meticulously organized, with grow beds arranged so everything got the proper sun it needed and all of the plants moving around each other almost like water. Vines were wrapped around tomato trellises, offering tethering support when the red fruit grew heavy and caused them to lean. Pepper plants provided shade for other gourds and melons as they crept along the ground. He could smell several different fresh herbs in the air, a distinct aroma that always made him think about summers at home.

"So she needs things watered here, and pruned and picked. Probably fertilized too? I used to try to help her with this when I was younger, but apparently, I have a black thumb 'cause I killed a whole bunch of stuff. This was kinda her and Dad's thing, so I'd hate to see it suffer on top of everything else. If this died... well, it would probably crush her.

"And there are people in town who rely on it for fresh food. We're not exactly in a food desert, but you know how it is when people get old. They get forgotten, get fed boring, bland stuff that's easy on their teeth. Teddy told me that sometimes she's the only person they see for days on end—because they've outlived everyone else they know, or their insurance messed up their home aid situation, or just because their families are working or sick."

Roman nodded, his expression turning resolute. "Yeah, you wanna help my sister? Take care of this garden for her. Hell, even I'll owe you one if you do that. I just... I really love her, but sometimes it's so hard to get into that head of hers, and I feel like I've been making her take care of my messes far too much lately."

Wow. He was obviously trying to downplay the situation,

but Silas could hear the emotion in the man's voice. Teddy's family really loved each other. With that warm, welcoming, accepting kind of love that sometimes Silas wondered if his family had at all.

"She loves you, you know." Maybe that was a weird thing to say, but it felt right. Because Silas knew for a fact, as sure as he knew about breathing, that Teddy loved her brother. And her father. And her community.

Roman let out a small laugh. "Oh, don't I know it. She'd go to the ends of the earth for Andre or me." Silas didn't miss how Roman's eyes lingered on him meaningfully. "I just wish there were more people willing to do the same for her."

Silas nodded, knowing exactly what the brother meant. Rolling up his sleeves, he looked over the space, recalling all the lessons his own mother had been giving him lately about the work a generous garden needed.

"Looks like I have my work cut out for me right now. But later, we're going to head to the nearest home improvement store. I'm starting to get some ideas."

18

Theodora

Teddy felt relief flow through her as Roman walked into Andre's hospital room, looking refreshed despite the fact that she had given his room to the kids and he had to sleep on the living room couch. She did feel a *wee* bit guilty about that, but she was sure her older brother understood. The whole Andre situation had her feeling all worried and protective. Like she wanted to hug all three of them and not let them go until Mrs. Merialda or maybe Ms. Beniot was free to watch them.

Of course, she couldn't really do that, so giving them a place to stay the night would have to be enough.

Andre had been mildly worried that the kids would end up doing something they shouldn't, especially considering all the heavy equipment and potentially dangerous tools they had lying around, so Roman had offered to stay the whole day there until they left. He'd stopped by the hospital to bring dinner, but then he went back home again for a good sleep and to do the laundry. Of course, since he was doing three people's worth of clothes, that pretty much took all of that day too, and Teddy had told him to stay at home. Sure, she missed her brother, but she could survive two and a half days away from him. Especially considering that he wasn't in jail this time.

But still, when he was supposed to arrive by lunch and ended up not strolling in until three, she would be lying if she denied that she was worried.

"Sorry I'm late," he said, not sounding sorry at all. "I got caught up in some stuff."

"Oh?" She surprised herself by wanting to know what was going on in the outside world. The first few days after she found her father unconscious on the floor, her whole world had revolved around him and his recovery. She'd been so scared that she was going to lose him, that she would have to watch another one of her parents die, that it seemed like there wasn't room for anything else in her brain. "Like what?"

"Just stuff. Finishing up the chores and all that you wanted me to do. How you feeling, Dad?"

Andre set his newspaper down, affixing them both with an irritated look. "I'm just *fine,* so you know. Just like I was just fine yesterday. And the day before that. I've been in the hospital for over a week. I am ready to go *home.*"

It was a speech that they had heard many times in the past few days. Roman nodded along. "Good to hear, Dad."

He looked back at Teddy, and she couldn't help but feel like her brother looked... excited? That was weird. Maybe she was misreading his energy after a good night's sleep. Goodness knew they both had been short on sleep ever since that night.

The hospital recliner and love seat weren't exactly the pinnacle of comfort.

"You should head home," Roman said.

"Why?" she asked suspiciously. "I took a shower this morning, so I know I don't smell that bad."

He chuckled lightly. "Nah, you smell fine. But I know you only washed and ate when you went back home. I bet you could pass out for a whole day if you tried."

Teddy looked uncertainly between her brother and father, but Andre nodded in agreement. "You two have wasted enough time around here. Go get some rest. I don't want you letting yourself get run-down on my account."

With both of them telling her to go, it was hard to resist the idea of her wonderfully warm bed back at home. "Fine, y'all win. I'll be back tomorrow morning. And *I* won't be late."

"Ouch, was that a dig at me?" Roman asked.

"Maybe," she said, sticking her tongue out. With a kiss to both of their cheeks and directions on where he parked the car, she left the hospital and headed back home. Despite her and her brother starting to take shifts, it'd still been five days since she'd slept in her own bed. She was more than ready for it.

When she pulled up to the shop, she was surprised to see how amazingly *clean* it was outside. Not that Andre ever let it get run down—it was his pride and joy, after all—but still, the business had its fair share of wear and tear. A couple of weeds growing around the edges, some of the paint at the top of their sign yellowed by the intense sun, some grit on the windows of their garage doors. But all of that was *gone*. And was that a completely new sign!?

Wow. Roman had really gone above and beyond. No wonder he was gone for practically three days straight.

Heading inside and up the stairs, she saw they had a new door at the top as well. Something that felt sturdier and was painted a solid-looking silver. When she slid her key into the lock, she was surprised that it slid in smoothly, allowing the door to swing open gently despite its weight.

Yet, despite that dramatic sort of entrance, it still didn't prepare her for what was waiting on the other side of the door.

Their old, worn furniture was all gone, replaced with newer and much less threadbare versions. She hadn't even realized the age of most of their furniture items until she saw newer ones in their place.

The couch was lush and soft to the touch, a deep sort of burgundy that fit in so well with the walls. There was a matching love seat as well, along with a low-coffee table and two side tables with fancy-looking lamps. A simple touch showed that they were *really* fancy lamps, the kind that had three levels of brightness that could be accessed with simply a tap.

"What is going on here?" she asked herself, heading over to the kitchen.

That was different too. She was facing all new appliances, shiny and chrome, and *very* impressive looking. It was like a home makeover from on TV, except she was on her own, staring at what seemed like an entirely new house instead of the apartment she had lived in since she was ten.

There was no way that Roman could have afforded all of it on his own so... she didn't know what that meant. But all of it seemed to be impossible.

Her phone buzzed, making her jump, and she pulled it out with shaking hands. Naturally, it was a text from Roman, and she could feel the cheekiness in the words there.

So, do you like it?

She couldn't believe it. Shaking her head, she quickly replied.

Of course! What's going on? How did you afford all of this?

I didn't. You know I'm broke.

Yeah, because you keep spending all your money on collectible Jays.

Whatever. Go enjoy your present.

This is crazy. It's not even Christmas.

Yeah, well I guess Santa felt like being real early. Or late I guess, depending on how ya look at it. Anyway, go enjoy.

You're crazy, you know that?

Stop lingering. Go enjoy the rest of the house. I know you ain't seen it all yet.

Rolling her eyes, she slid her phone back into her pocket. She couldn't believe this was happening. Was she actually trapped in some sort of hyper-realistic dream? She was beginning to wonder. Feeling like she was on another planet, she headed to the back part of their apartment. There was only one door open, so she found herself heading right toward the bathroom.

"Oh, my goodness," she said when it all came into view. And even that exclamation didn't do it justice.

The entire bathroom had been completely redone. Top to bottom. There was a deep tub now with a standing shower right next to it—where their simple shower had been— complete with a regular shower head and a detachable shower head on the opposite side.

The sink was also redone, taking up less room but with a fancier cabinet under it. And the mirror? That was new too, twice as big and split into three sections. A simple press to the corner of each section revealed the built-in medicine cabinet behind each one, and an LED strip around the edges made it perfect for doing makeup in.

Wow.

Wow.

Everything from the window curtains, to the shower curtains, to the rug on the floor was new and meticulously thought of, making the whole space look bigger and feel warmer.

"This... this is amazing," she said. She pinched herself to make sure that it was real, and sure enough, the room stayed the same.

No wonder Roman had asked to switch with her and kept her in the hospital for two and a half days. But still, she was amazed that he had been able to do so much in only forty-eight hours.

Except...

There was no way Roman would have been able to afford even a quarter of the stuff on his own, and while he was incredibly good with engines, that didn't extend to plumbing or painting or any of the other things necessary for what had changed.

But if he hadn't done it on his own, she only really knew a single person who had the kind of liquid capital to afford everything that she had seen.

Well, a single *family*.

She stood there, shocked by the idea. Could Silas have really helped fund the total makeover for her living space? Why would he do that? She already owed him so much money. And yet, that was the only answer that made sense.

She would have to text later. Whether it was to ask him if he was on some sort of drug or to thank him was yet to be determined. But first, she wanted to take that luxurious looking tub for a spin.

She actually did an excited Frenchie-clap and squeal before quickly filling the bathtub up. When she grabbed for her toiletries bag under the new, fancy sink, she was surprised to see that that was restocked too. There was no way her brother paid attention to what kind of bath bombs she liked, so that definitely meant he had help.

But was that something Silas would notice? That seemed to make sense, but also made her stomach flutter in a way she wasn't used to.

Shoving that thought aside, she slid into the bath, watching as the water rose, then plopped the pretty bomb right in.

Ahhh, relaxation. She spent much longer than she should have soaking, nearly dozing, but when she got out, she felt restored in a way she hadn't expected. In fact, she felt strong enough to go check on the carnage that would be her garden.

She'd asked Roman to water it, but that was about all she trusted him to do. She loved her brother dearly, but whatever genes made Andre good with plants had absolutely skipped over his son. The guy could kill a succulent in days flat, even with her careful guidance. She didn't get it.

Wrapping herself in the fluffy, baby blue bathrobe that was hanging on the back of the bathroom door, she put on her slippers and headed back downstairs. She wasn't worried about anyone spotting her in her comfy getup considering the privacy fence, and it was just so nice to not be in a jumpsuit or three-day-old sweats.

She had been expecting overgrowth and maybe some deaths from overwatering, but that wasn't what waited for her at all. From the moment she opened the door, she was acutely aware that something was different.

First of all, her garden was actively being watered by a series of automatic sprinklers, and a quick glance around saw a control panel on the wall. They were a series of small pipes above the ground—because anything else would have required digging up her garden—but there were brightly colored bands on the lengths so she wouldn't trip.

The plants had all been properly trimmed. She saw that new trellises had been put in where her old, popsicle ones had been nearly bending under the strain. Her tomato cages looked new too, while the half-shells of the old one all stood in a neat row, supporting the beans that had clung to it.

It was... it was *beautiful.* And it was all for her. No one else really cared about the garden like she did, not even Andre. So, if it really was Silas who had done everything, he'd done it specifically for *her.*

That thought made her breath catch. She stood there for several moments, looking at the beauty of it all.

Maybe, just maybe, she had a lot to think about once everything calmed down.

Her stomach rumbled, interrupting the rather emotional moment and startling a laugh from her chest. Taking one last look at the beautiful spread of green and life, she headed back in to make herself a *very* carby dinner. She'd certainly earned it.

Besides, it was always easier to process feelings on a full stomach.

TEDDY WAS STILL FLOATING, as if in a dream, several hours later. She'd texted her brother, further reiterating how insane he was for orchestrating everything with Silas, but that was about it. She knew she needed to message Silas eventually. But she wanted to thank him as enthusiastically as she felt, and every time she started to text, she felt like she didn't have the right words to convey how amazing everything was. And when she thought of calling him to say it that way, her mouth went dry and her heart started to do a full conga line impression.

So instead, she sat on the couch in her fuzzy robe and slippers, feet up on the new, lush ottoman, and she watched one of her favorite movies on the DVD player.

All in all, it was the nicest night she'd had since before Andre had collapsed, and she felt totally spoiled.

So when the buzzer sounded downstairs, she didn't even mind. Maybe it would be Antonio or one of the others come to check up on her. That would be lovely. Maybe she could show them around the house, and they would agree to watch a movie with her. She could even feed them all. After being taken care of so thoughtfully, she was definitely in the mood to spread it around. She kind of wished she could hug the whole neighborhood; she was so syrupy and contented inside. Her father was on the mend, her family was together, and she had the best kinda employer she could ever ask for.

Heading down, she glanced out of the peephole to see it was one of the younger girls she saw very rarely. Amarillis? Esme? She couldn't quite remember the name, but she did recall that the girl was dating one of the wannabe gangsters that was *far* too old for her. She looked roughed up, as the teens who visited her door often were, so Teddy quickly opened the door.

"Hey, are you al—" Teddy started to say.

But suddenly it wasn't only the girl there. Others stepped in from either side of the door, roughly shoving Teddy back.

She stumbled, surprised by the sudden company, and clutched at her bathrobe. She wished she had put something else on as they crowded her further into the shop, more of them appearing until there were six of them and the girl.

Somehow, in her quick recovery, she managed to grab the baseball bat above the door on instinct. She hadn't even been aware that she had done it until she came to a stop and the smooth, tapered wood of the handle was in her hand. Blinking quickly, she brought it up as a warning, facing the group.

She knew the young men in her space. All of them. They were the gang that her family had never gotten along with. The same ones that she had chased off of Silas that one night that seemed like ages ago.

"Good evening," their leader said. "We heard that your pa's been sick. Real sorry 'bout that."

She forced herself to stand straight. Like she wasn't in an enclosed space wearing nothing but a fuzzy robe and slippers. She'd fought plenty in her life, sure, because she was a scrapper, but she knew when she was outnumbered. Sure, she had the home-field advantage, but that hardly meant anything when there were six of them and just one of her.

"I'll pass along your condolences. Now, if you don't mind, Eugene, I'd like to get some rest."

"That ain't my name," the young man hissed, his cheeks instantly coloring.

"What are you talking about, Eugene? That's absolutely your name. You're named after your father, ain't you?"

She knew that the young man didn't like his government name, that he insisted that everyone call him by the street name that he had made up. She also knew that she shouldn't be goading him, and yet that was exactly what she was doing. She really couldn't resist kicking the hornet's nest, could she?

"Shut up. You don't know anything about me. But I do know that this shop been real busy the past few days. That fancy-pants outsider you saved been around and doin' a whole lot." He nodded to the others and spread out. Teddy lifted her baseball bat to be on the offensive, warning them off, but none of them tried to go near her.

Instead they went to the peripherals of her vision, smashing windows and knocking over toolboxes. The first shatter surprised her, making her jump, and the second made her want to sob. But she didn't allow any of that to pass beyond her brain. She didn't want these young men to think they were getting to her. Because if they did, they would only escalate.

"So what's the deal? You turn down one shark just to hop in bed with another? Yeah, I bet that's exactly what you did, didn't you?"

She didn't miss the double entendre of his words. Tension coiled around her back, radiating out to her legs. "We haven't sold to anybody, and we never will."

"You sure about that? You know, this neighborhood's getting dangerous and your pa ain't getting younger."

More shatters. More crashing. The five others were breaking everything they could get their hands on and upturning anything they couldn't. Every single bit of damage felt like it went right through her heart, ripping out a chunk of her and leaving it smeared across the floor. But she couldn't show them that. She had to be *strong*. Impervious.

The leader continued, "Maybe you should do the smart thing and get out of here while the going is good. I'm sure that Mr. Cartwright is willing to make a real good deal."

That startled her, pulling her mind away from the destruction around her. "How do you know his name?"

Eugene shrugged. "I'm a businessman. I make it my business to know other professionals."

"Oh," she said, a feeling bite to her words. "And is that what you are? A professional?"

Suddenly he was up in her space, sneering down at her. Teddy was by no means a wilting flower, but she was acutely aware of how much *bigger* the young man was than her. If she didn't have the baseball bat, would he be laying hands on her? *Was* he going to lay hands on her?

Eugene's eyes grew darker. "You always been so uppity, you know that? You and your whole family think you're better than us because you got this business. But you ain't nothing. *Nothing.*"

She knew that she should be quiet, that she should let him say his piece and go. But some part of her was never willing to lie low and let people walk all over her.

"Huh, that's a whole lot of nothing you're breaking around here then. And I guess our insurance will be paying us more money than you'll see in a year over all this nothing. But if that's the case, and we're nothing, that means you and your whole lot are... what?" She pretended to ponder. "Less than nothing, I guess."

He spat a curse at her and, the next thing she knew, his hand was flying toward her to slap her across the face. She blocked it with her bat, then turned the wood to jab the butt into his stomach. Eugene coughed and doubled over, but then one of the others was rushing past him to shove her harshly backward.

She went with the momentum, keeping her eyes on them, bat still raised. They'd stopped breaking things, so that was something, but now the entire crowd was staring at her with no undue amount of ill intent in their eyes.

"Same thing as last time," she heard herself say much more steadily than she felt. "I can't take all of you, but I'm gonna take at least half of you. If you wanna play those odds, step right up."

There was a moment of hesitation like they were thinking about exactly those odds. Their eyes narrowed. With one more person added to their number, they weren't nearly as scared as before. Or maybe it was because she was only dressed in a bathrobe and Silas wasn't there to be backup. She was acutely aware of all the differences that put her at a disadvantage, and she was sure that they were too.

Then the tension snapped, and she could tell they were about to rush forward. She crouched, but before any could make it to her, the garage doors started to open on their own and the place was flooded with blinding lights. Sirens soon split the air, sounding urgent and accusatory in their shrieking.

"This is the police. Stop all activity and drop any weapons. Do not move!"

There was a series of curses and cries to get out. Teddy

shielded her eyes, straining to listen, but her adrenaline was making her blood rush past her ears. The cacophony seemed to last forever until it suddenly wasn't there anymore, and the lights cut out.

She had to blink the light spots away for several moments, and even before her vision came all the way back, she felt a gentle hand touch her arm.

"Hey there, are you alright?"

She flinched automatically before her ears caught up with her brain. She knew that voice!

"Silas?"

"Yeah, I'm here. You alright? Can you see? I'm sorry for blinding you, but I wanted to make sure that they didn't see it was just me."

She couldn't stop herself and she didn't want to; she hugged him, holding onto him so tightly she was sure that she heard his back pop. But he didn't object and let her hold him as long as she needed.

Which turned out to be about two full minutes, and when she let go, she could finally see without little spots dancing in front of her eyes.

"How did you even do that?" she asked. "It really sounded like there was a whole armada out there."

At that he chuckled. "Just my car's brights plus the fog lights and a Bluetooth connection to my phone to play some police sirens from online. Technology really is a wonder, isn't it?"

She laughed too, but it was a much more panicked sound than she would have liked. "Yeah, I'd say so."

"Do you have any weatherproof plastic? Or garbage bags? I'll cover up the windows, and you can head upstairs."

"Leave it. They're not going to come back today with that

stunt you pulled. I'll report everything in the morning, and we can clean it up then. For now, I just don't want to be alone."

He shot her a warm grin, apparently not thinking her request was bizarre or pathetic. "Sure. We can do that."

He took her hand and led her upstairs, gently picking around all the mess. It was going to be a task and a half to clean it up the next day, but it would get done. What mattered to Teddy at the moment was feeling safe.

Because she had been feeling so safe, warm and protected before those hoodlums had arrived. She knew she wouldn't be able to get back to exactly that, but she wanted to try. Because if she didn't calm down soon, she felt like she might rattle apart entirely.

They made it up to the new and improved living room, and he walked her over to the couch before going back to lock the entrance securely. Once he was done, he came back to her and gave her an uncertain look.

"How can I help? A glass of water?"

She nodded, realizing her mouth was as dry as the desert. "Yeah, that would be nice."

"Ice or no ice? Your fridge has a filter now, by the by, and it comes cold right out of the door."

Teddy managed a weak chuckle. "You really did all this, didn't you?"

He flushed, and if that wasn't just the most dashing look across his broad features. "I hope it's not too jarring. I just wanted to help."

"Oh, you helped alright," she said, taking the cool glass he offered her when he returned. "I... I have no idea how I'm ever going to repay this."

"Please don't," he said quickly, then flushed again when he realized how urgently he'd said it. "I mean, it was a gift.

People don't have to pay back gifts. That defeats the purpose."

"I suppose you may have a point." She drank about half the water then gave him an uncertain look. "Do you have to go right now?"

"No. I could stick around. Do you need anything else?"

Could she say that she needed him? No, that was far too much. Crossing too many lines. "We could watch a movie? That would be nice."

"You want to watch a movie with me?"

She nodded. "If it's not too much trouble."

"It wouldn't be trouble at all."

More relief flooded through her. She could certainly use it considering the emotional roller coaster her day had been. Patting the spot next to her on the couch, she scooted over so that he could be comfortable. But not *that* far over. She wasn't a saint, after all.

"I don't suppose you refilled our cupboards on top of remodeling our whole apartment, did you?"

"Actually, I did have one of my workers grab a few things since I figured you'd be too tired to cook. Do you want pretzels or pizza bites?"

"Is that even a contest? Pizza bites. Definitely."

"Alright then. I'll be right back."

He returned to the kitchen and, true to his word, he did return with snacks and more cool drinks. Without any fanfare, he sat on the couch beside her as she started up her movie again from the beginning.

It felt nice, having him next to her. Warm and solid. She could feel him looking at her from time to time, but he never made her talk. It seemed that he was just as content as her to sit there, enjoying the nostalgia of the movie.

But when it ended, she wasn't ready for him to go. She didn't want to be alone with the mess of a shop downstairs and the fear of exactly what lengths Mr. Cartwright was willing to go. So, she asked if he'd watch another movie with her.

And to her great surprise, Silas said yes.

So, they sat through that too, drink and pizza bites long gone, just watching and being in the moment together. But good things could only last for so long because then that was over too, and she was sleepily looking over at the handsome man.

Wow, she was exhausted. Without all that adrenaline pumping through her, she felt like a hollowed-out log.

"It's late. I suppose I should let you go."

He let out a truly massive yawn, then rose to stand. "Alright, if you're done for the night—" Silas didn't finish his sentence, and that was probably because she was gripping his arm tightly, fear pinging around inside of her skull all over again. But instead of looking irritated with her, his face softened again.

"You know, I'm not sure I'm awake enough to make the hour-plus drive home. If you don't mind, I can crash on the couch."

Of course, he would make it like *he* was asking *her* a favor. Because he was kind and sweet and entirely out of her league like that.

"Would you?" she asked in a voice much smaller than the one she would normally use. But he didn't comment on that either.

"Absolutely."

19

───────

Silas

Silas woke up slowly, consciousness rolling over him in doleful waves. The first thing he realized was that there was a massive crick in his neck, quickly followed up by the fact that he smelled something absolutely delicious.

Both were motivating him to sit up, which he did with a groan. After a quick crack of his neck to ease the tension, the situation came rushing back to him.

He was at Teddy's. Her shop had been razzed the last night, a harsh counterpoint to the happiness that she was supposed to get from the remodel of her apartment. He hated that those creeps had scared her, but he also hated that they had tainted something he'd been so excited to give her. True, the apartment hadn't been touched by the gang members, and for that he was grateful, but there was always going to be that shadow on the day.

At least it seemed that she liked things, judging by the truly oversized, thick and fuzzy bathrobe she was wearing. It was one of the things he'd seen online during the first day, and he'd rush shipped it to make sure it arrived in time.

He had almost thought their project wasn't going to work out. He'd paid a ridiculous amount of money to hire some of the on-call construction guys and designers his family had, and even more money to do things as quickly as they had, nearly two dozen men working in shifts around the clock. Silas had wanted to do more, but the professionals had been very clear about what was just insane and what was physically impossible.

The smell of caramelized bacon curled around his nose, reminding him of part of what had woken him up. Standing, he brushed himself off and traveled the short distance to the kitchen. It was still quite small to him, but at least they had a dishwasher and lovely appliances to make up for it. While coin could work some wonders, it couldn't make the inside bigger than the outside.

No, he needed a British police box for that, and those were in short supply.

But he wasn't quite ready for what was waiting for him. Teddy was standing at the stove, cooking up a storm.

It wasn't the what she was *doing* so much as what she was *wearing* as she did it. It wasn't that she was in anything scandalous, but it certainly wasn't a mechanic's jumpsuit either. She was wearing a pretty lilac camisole, all satin looking, paired with soft, yellow shorts that looked like they were made out of some sort of cotton or other natural fiber.

He tried not to look at her legs, but it was difficult, especially considering how pale they were in the kitchen light. She had bright blue polish on her toenails. Now that was something he hadn't expected.

"Oh hey, you're up. I was just making breakfast. Then I'm going to report the break-in."

"The break-in?"

"Yeah, that was what I was going to call it. I'll tell them the truth, but I might leave out some... details."

He sat down at the table, telling himself to stop staring at her before he grew creepy or inappropriate. "What kind of details."

He didn't miss the slight hesitance before she answered. "Nothing too important. Just, maybe, that it might have been Mr. Cartwright that sent them."

Now *that* jolted him, his knee coming up to bang against the bottom of the table. "He *what*!?"

"I can't say for sure, and I don't have any proof, but I'm almost certain."

Silas tried hard to bite his tongue, but he was fuming. He knew that Cartwright was a scumbag, but that was so far over the line he was practically in another country. "What makes you so certain?"

"Something Eugene said. He basically spelled it out for me. The only question is if he was telling the truth or if he was just trying to scare me even further. I think I believe it, though. After what Cartwright did to my brother, I don't put much of anything past him."

Silas hadn't lost his temper in a long while, but he felt it bubbling up, wild and untamed within him. The thought that someone in *his* circle could stoop so low—could try to *hurt* Teddy just for gain.

"I... I'm going to go clean up the shop," Silas said.

"What? But I haven't finished breakfast! And the cops have to take pictures of everything for insurance, I'm sure."

"Right. *Right.*" He took a deep breath. He needed to calm down. It wouldn't do any good at all if he lost his head right in front of Teddy. So, he buried his anger, telling himself that he would get to address it, he would, but it wasn't the right moment.

"Besides, what does it matter?" she asked, shrugging as she returned to the oven.

But that ticked something in Silas. "What do you mean, what does it matter?"

She shrugged again, her posture defensive. "It's all a cycle. Used to happen about every five years or so. Now it's happening faster and faster because of greed. Because of—"

"Gentrification," he supplied, and she sighed like she was relieved he understood her.

"Yes, exactly, that. Mr. Cartwright is very good at understanding how to play us, how to pick at our weaknesses. He's the smartest, I think, of all of those who have attempted so far.

"And that's all it takes, really. You try and you try to fight, to dig your roots in, but in the end, it really only takes one really smart wolf out of all the wolves to wheedle their way in."

He hated how resigned she sounded; it wasn't like his Teddy. Not that she was ever really *his*, but the point still stood.

Silas couldn't hold back all of his anger. "But it's *wrong*. All of this is wrong! People shouldn't be chased from their homes when they've already said no!" He found himself striding forward, gesturing emphatically. "They shouldn't have gang members sent after them, to invade their homes. To break things! What would they have done to you if I hadn't been there? It's all—"

Suddenly she whipped around, her eyes full of fire as she regarded him. For the third time, it brought them surprisingly close together, and his steam quickly petered out.

"You talk so pretty, and about these values, but wasn't your family intending to do the very same?"

Her voice was quiet, but deceptively so. He could hear the steel to it, strong and unbreakable.

"*No.* It's not like that at all. We wouldn't—"

"Wouldn't you?" she interrupted. "Or has anyone ever refused you? The big, strong Miller empire—with all its riches—makes an intimidating foe. A foe most wouldn't want to have against them at all." She took a step closer until they were basically chest to chest. "I want to believe you, but some back part of my mind keeps telling me that you're not mad about what's happening, but only that you're mad that he's better at the game than you."

That was perhaps the last thing he expected out of her mouth. After everything he had done for her, that was how she still saw him.

"What do I have to do to prove to you I'm not like that?"

The fire in her eyes dimmed, and she turned away from him. "The shadow of your family is over me, and although you're a nicer fate, although I *like* you, it lingers all the same. After this issue with Cartwright is gone, after my contract is up, can you assure me that your enterprise won't sweep in and pick up the pieces?"

Silas wanted to tell her no; he wanted to yell it from the roof. But then the logical part of his mind kicked in and he realized that no, he couldn't say anything of the sort. Because the truth was, if his dad ordered it, the acquisition would move right along. Silas had already supplied all the information he needed.

"I'm..." He paused, took a breath. "I'm going to make this right," he announced before turning heel and heading out.

He had his work cut out for him.

20

____

Silas

Silas didn't know the office locations of every frenemy his dad had, but he did know how to look them up. And that was exactly how he ended up striding right into the office of none other than Philip Rupert Cartwright and his associates, with Solomon and several of their lawyers right behind him.

The receptionist stood, asking if they had a meeting, but he brushed right past her. Security hadn't stopped them, if only because they recognized the Millers after years of interactions, so what hope did the small woman in heels armed with only a hole punch and a calendar have?

Silas slammed the door open probably harder than was necessary, and he relished the shocked look on Philip's weaselly face as the whole party made their way in.

"Sam, what's going on here?"

"It's Silas," he corrected, crossing over to the man's overly ostentatious desk. "You're well aware of that."

"Am I?" The man's lips curled into a sort of mocking grin. "Sorry if it's so hard to tell you lot apart. A whole clan of cowboys playing as businessmen: surely you can understand my trouble keeping you lot straight."

"Funny, coming from the middle son of a middling family who owns a middling company that's falling apart from... where exactly?" Silas leaned down, pressing both of his hands on the man's desk. He knew he was getting fingerprints on the wood, and that was exactly what he wanted. "Ah, right. Falling apart from the middle of things."

"Our company is doing fine."

"Is that so?" Sterling asked from behind Silas, his voice as cold as ice. One of the things his younger twin could always do better was to sound borderline threatening without saying anything legally actionable at all. "If that's the case, then why have you been harassing multiple members of the community?"

The man snorted and sat back, looking incredulous. "Oh, is *that* what this little display is all about? And here I thought something important had happened while I wasn't paying attention." He shook his head. "You needn't worry about our development projects. There's plenty of pie in our city for both of us."

"And does that pie include you trying to use the cops and sicking gang members on innocent civilians?"

"Gang members? I have no idea what you're talking about."

Silas slammed his palms down, making a loud boom but keeping his face perfectly calm. "Don't play coy. I have one of the members on a recording confessing that you've been backing them and sent them to scare out the Parker family.

Caused a *lot* of physical damage to the shop. That's illegal, you know."

It was a bluff, but Cartwright didn't know that. And if there was one thing he had learned from playing both Uno and Texas Hold'Em with his brothers, it was how to keep one heck of a poker face.

"Please, like you couldn't have just hired any one of those urchins to make up any story you wanted. If it's going to be my word against theirs, who do you think they're gonna believe."

That made Silas burn. If only because he was right. It was like Teddy had inferred multiple times. People like him didn't have to follow the same rules that folks like her did. It wasn't right, but if Silas was forced to play that game, he was going to make sure he used his power to help even things out.

"You're right. Or at least, you would be, if I hadn't been there myself to witness the entire thing. I even saw one of them put their hands on the daughter. You remember her, right? Red hair, pretty face, big eyes. The kind that will make a jury feel a particular sympathy when they hear about the middle son of a slumlord trying to ice her out."

Finally, the man looked as nervous as he needed to be. He licked his lips, his face going pale. "You were there?"

"Oh yeah. I even got to catch them on my cell phone, running away, tail tucked between their legs."

The man's hands fluttered for a moment, like he wasn't certain what to do with them, before he took a steadying breath.

"Alright. What do you want?"

"We want you to drop whatever plans you have for the neighborhood. I don't care where you have to go, find some-where else."

"That's out of my hands—"

Silas leaned forward further, staring down the scum of a man. "Then get it *in* your hands. And I want you to drop all the charges you have against the young Parker son."

"Is that all?"

"No. I want you to pay for the repairs on the shop, and cover if their insurance goes up at all."

He swallowed, seeming to realize how serious the situation was. "Fine. I agree to your terms. And you agree to drop this and delete your evidence file?"

"One more thing," Solomon said, his voice almost as chilly as Sterling's had been. "You stop all interaction with the gang. And if any of us ever get news of you meddling with any of them again, we'll leak all of this to some particularly ravenous journalists who would love to take a bite out of one of the one percent of our city."

"Yes, yes. Whatever. I agree. Get you and your lawyers out of here if you want me to do anything about the development."

"That's my man, Philip. I always love it when our families play ball." Silas gave him an amiable grin like he hadn't just threatened the crap out of the man, then stood. "Shall we?" he asked, turning to his brothers and their team.

"You know," Sterling said casually, all of the ice gone from his tone. "I'm really jonesing for some pancakes. Think there's a diner around here with all-day breakfast?"

"I'm sure we'll be able to find something," Silas said with a laugh as they all headed out.

Pride swelled in Silas' chest as they exited, stopping on the sidewalk to organize. If anything was going to convince Teddy that he wasn't another one of the sharks, that he wasn't there for acquisition, he had done it. He just hoped that his sense of accomplishment wasn't premature.

"Hey, you guys all head to the diner, I'll be there in a minute. I have a call to make."

"Of course," Sterling said, hands in his pockets. "Gotta tell your girlfriend that you totally saved her bacon, right?"

"She's not my girlfriend."

"*Ehhh*, you say potato, I say you're full of it."

"If she was my girlfriend, I'd like to think that maybe you wouldn't flirt with her right in front of my face."

Sterling shot him a cocky grin. "Touchy, aren't we? Look, if you're not going to make a move, I will. Girl is easy on the eyes and handy too. Not to mention she's got kinda that smoky voice thing going on that I dig."

"Who says I'm not going to make a move?"

"You, historically speaking. What, it's been since college since you've even tried, right? When what was her name? Marigold? Yeah, back when Marigold broke your heart."

"Marigold didn't break my heart. I've been busy."

"Busy for seven years?"

"Look, drop it, alright?"

He held up his hands, every bit the infuriating younger twin that he was so good at being. "Fine, fine. But I'm not gonna wait in the wings forever. Either finish or get off the pot, so to speak."

Silas rolled his eyes. "Fine. Whatever. Just let me make my phone call, alright?"

"Sure, whatever you want."

Finally, his brother walked off, and Silas pulled out his phone to dial Teddy. He was worried she might not answer, but to his immense alleviation, she did on the second ring.

"If you're calling to ask if you can still have breakfast, I ate it all and took the rest to my brother and father."

Oh, he probably deserved that. "I understand. I was hoping

that maybe we could talk? There are some things I need to update you on."

She let out a long sigh. "Not today. I'm bringing my dad home and I want him to rest. Tomorrow, I think. Tomorrow would be good."

"That's fine with me," Silas said, trying not to sound too eager. He'd also been worried that she wouldn't want to see him at all. "I have some other details I want to hash out first anyway."

"Alright. I'll see you then."

And hopefully when they did meet up, he'd have everything taken care of.

21

Theodora

*T*eddy's phone rang once, and she decided to let it go to voicemail as she finished cooking her grilled cheese. She knew that Silas was going to drop by and, after their conversation in the kitchen, she was already apprehensive.

He'd done *so* much for her. Why had she gone and thrown his richness in his face? It wasn't like he asked to be born into the family that was so rich. He didn't purposefully pop out a millionaire with his own private trust fund.

And hadn't he been kind to her? Helped her brother? Remodeled her whole place? Hadn't he proven that he wasn't one of the sharks?

Well... yes, but that was the crux of things, wasn't it? Even with him doing all of those things, they still put her further and further into his debt. She was his *employee*, his debtor, and no matter how wonderful and handsome he was, there was unequal ground there. And unequal ground was dangerous.

That was what her mother had taught her, if nothing else.

Her mom had been so young when she'd moved to Texas, running away from her own mother who liked the bottle too much and groceries not enough. She'd gotten the only job she could land, a cashier at one of the local shops. When her boss first started flirting with her, it was new and exciting, and before she knew it, she was swept up in a relationship.

A relationship that quickly grew sour. Teddy's mom had tried to protect her from finding out certain things, but people talked. About how the manager had a history of roping in pretty young girls. Of how he showered them with favors and compliments and attention until they were so enamored with him that they let him push the boundaries way farther than what they were truly comfortable with. He'd done exactly that to her mother, taking her out to a drive-in movie that turned out to be anything but.

And two months later, when her mom had first realized that she was pregnant with Teddy, she'd gone to the man asking how he was going to support his child. He'd thrown a fit, then soon left town. Teddy knew that there was a lot written between the lines there. Heartbreak, fights, screaming and pain. She knew there were abhorrent details that her mother didn't want to get out. To anyone.

If she were alive, if the cancer hadn't taken her away when Teddy was only ten years old, then she would be right next to her daughter explaining to her that trust wasn't something that could be bought and sold. As long as she was indentured to the Millers, as long as her brother's freedom and her shop's livelihood depended on those people not flexing their claws and sinking in their teeth, she couldn't ever let her guard fully down.

Even if she wholeheartedly, *desperately* wanted to.

But then her phone was ringing again, barely a moment after it had stopped. Ignoring one call was one thing, but if someone was double calling her, then it was probably something important.

Wiping her hands on her apron, she reached over and grabbed her cell. A quick swipe showed that it was the lawyer calling so she hurriedly answered it.

"Hello?" she asked cautiously, expecting bad news. It was never a good thing when a lawyer called out of the blue.

"Hi, Ms. Parker?"

"Yeah, it's me."

"I left a message with your brother already, but he expressed to me earlier that he wants all updates on his case shared with you, so I'm calling to let you know that all charges against your brother have been dropped."

She let out a strangled sort of sound, her heart practically leaping into her throat. "They *what?*"

"Dropped all of the charges. It's still being processed, but the additional good news is that your bail will be returned in full. I don't know if you need me to tell you this, but that means that your contract with the Millers has been paid in full. In addition, the contract states that you will personally be administered a refund for any services you rendered to the Miller family over the amount borrowed."

Teddy felt weak and had to lean against the counter, her face burning brightly. "I... are you for real?"

"Of course, Ms. Parker. I wouldn't joke about anything of that nature."

"I—"

Roman's voice interrupted. "Hey sis, look who pulled up as I came back from my walk?"

With uncanny timing, Roman came in, a nervous-looking Silas right behind him.

Everything had just changed, hadn't it?

"Thank you," Teddy said to the lawyer, barely remembering that she was supposed to speak. "I appreciate everything you've done for my family."

"Of course, Ms. Parker. You have a lovely day now."

"You know? I think I just might do that."

She hung up and turned slowly to Silas, so many thoughts sparking through her head that she almost felt dizzy. She didn't owe him anything. She wasn't employed by him at all. What had happened?

"Oh, um, it kinda seems like you two might wanna talk to each other," Roman said. "I'm gonna head right back out to get some smoothies from the corner store. You want anything?"

"Passionfruit guava," Teddy said, surprised that her brain was able to spit that out.

"Alright, I'll be back in ten minutes." He looked back and forth between the two of them then cleared his throat. "Actually, maybe fifteen."

It probably would have been comical if it was any other situation, but Teddy's heart was beating far too hard within her chest.

"The lawyer called me," she said simply. She didn't have any other words for it.

"Good. That's good." He stepped into the house, looking nervous. How funny to think that a girl like her could make someone like *him* nervous. "I wanted to tell you that scumbag won't be bothering you anymore. And my family will no longer be trying to buy up the area for our distribution center.

"However, we are interested in setting up a sort of community outreach building for events and other things. Somewhere where you all can come together and celebrate or use in case of emergencies."

"Why would you do that?" she asked. Her whole life she had been sure of how things worked and what she could expect from which people. But he was turning all of that on its head.

"Because I'm certain that that's the right thing to do. And I want to start doing the right thing whenever I can."

"I..."

Another step toward her. "Teddy, you are a good person, possibly the best I've ever met, and you've opened my eyes to a bunch of things."

"Things like what?" she said. The way he was looking at her just wasn't fair. It made her *feel* things. Things that she had been trying so desperately not to acknowledge.

"Things like personal responsibility. And community. And how much privilege I have for just being a Miller. And also..."

He took another step toward her, purposefully bringing them closer together. It wasn't like all those accidental times where they ended up right on top of each other. It was purposeful. And *boy*, was her body reacting to it.

Silas took her hands in his. "Because I'd like to take you on a date, and I couldn't do any of that when there was all that paperwork between us. We needed to start on the same footing. You know, equal ground."

She was in absolute shock. She must have misheard him! Surely that couldn't have been what he had said. But then he was speaking again, looking at her with that *look* that really should come with some sort of medical warning.

"You're beautiful. You're strong. You're, frankly, amazing.

And I know I've taken some missteps since we've known each other, but if you could see it in you to let me take you on a date, I'd be much obliged."

Perhaps she stared at him longer than she should have before realizing that she needed to say something. She absolutely needed to say something.

"I think I could be amenable to that."

"Oh, you think so?"

She couldn't stop the broad grin that crossed her face, and she didn't want to. "Yeah, I think so."

22

Teddy

A text buzzed on her phone, and a quick check told her that it was Silas announcing that he had arrived. She didn't need the notice, however, because she was standing at their front door, looking out at the street.

She bounded out quickly, wearing a comfortable but cute outfit. It was weirdly early on a Saturday morning, but it was when Silas had wanted to pick her up, so she had agreed.

She couldn't believe that she was going on a date with him. After over a month of beating herself up and telling herself that they were from different realms of existence, it turned out that he had felt the same way about her.

Uncanny. Impossible. And yet? Actually happening.

Of course, there was still that voice in the back of her head, the one that whispered that she couldn't trust him, that he was too rich, too spoiled, too close to what had almost upheaved her life. She mentally told that voice to shut up more than once, but it was persistent.

Probably because he was so unlike anyone else she knew. No one in her life would have been able to just casually bail out her brother or remodel their home to make her feel better. He was like a Prince Charming from a book, but she was acutely aware that that kind of thing wasn't real.

But if it wasn't real, did that mean he was faking? And if he was faking, did that mean he would grow bored with her? Get her all warm and comfortable and reliant on him, then disappear in a flash? That was what rich guys did, right?

She shook her head as she hopped into the vehicle while Silas held the door open for her. Since when had she grown so untrusting? Had she always been that way? She shouldn't. People had been generous to her most of her life. Helping out her mother when things were hard, helping out her mother again when the cancer came back. And eventually helping Teddy herself when she didn't have a mom anymore.

Maybe it was just the fact that he was an outsider. As a rule, outsiders were people to watch out for. They didn't get her. Didn't get her family. Or maybe it was that he looked so similar to the people who had been causing their neighborhood headaches since long before she was born.

"You ready for today?" he asked, all smiles as she buckled up.

Teddy couldn't help the guilt that flashed through her. After weeks pining for him, she finally had a shot at the man, so why was she suddenly so locked up in her own skull? It was like she was trying to purposefully sabotage her own happiness.

"Are you finally going to tell me where it is that we're going?"

He pursed his lips and rubbed his chin as if he were debating it, before punching the location into the GPS. "Well, I figure the standard is dinner and a movie, but we've already done that in a sort of backhanded way, so I wanted to do something special."

"Right, because remodeling our whole apartment wasn't special."

"That was a gift just because you deserved it. It's separate from courting you."

She felt herself falling back into their usual banter, and it was such a relief. "Oh, so we're courting now?"

"We will be if you let me go ahead and finish my sentence."

Teddy laughed at that, those dark thoughts edging back from the front of her mind. "Alright, alright. Where are we headed?"

"I thought it might be fun to go to the Dallas Arboretum and Botanical Gardens. It's a bit of a drive, but sounds worth it, doesn't it?"

Teddy had to hold back her surprised gasp, feeling like it would sound more sarcastic than genuine. "I haven't been there since I was a kid. I loved it there." If she closed her eyes, she could still see the beautiful plants, smell the wonderful aroma of flowers and ferns and all the wonderful foliage. Fresh earth and water, even the large ponds full of koi. All of it was wonderful, borderline magical in her head.

"Ah, so I picked good?"

"You picked *very* good," she said. How could she doubt him when he was so thoughtful? When he so very obviously wanted to make this something special for their first date. It was unlike how anybody else had ever treated her. Ever tried to date her.

But what if it was all just a front?

She rolled her eyes at herself. *Really?* Couldn't she just enjoy the wonderful moment?

She wasn't used to being so on edge around a person. Normally people were so easy to read, but she couldn't help but feel that Silas functioned by an entirely different set of rules that she'd never heard of.

IT WOULD BE A VERY Teddy thing if she managed to ruin everything all on her own. She needed to get over the uncertainty that was constantly bringing her thoughts down.

She looked out the window, trying to center herself, and it helped that the drive, in and of itself, was rather soothing. He had some sort of old country music playing softly on the radio, turned down so that he could point out different landmarks and funny stories about them. She appreciated the anecdotes, connecting together more about his life.

By the time they arrived, she'd managed to calm down for the most part, but a lot of her doubts sank down to settle in her stomach, making her feel like she had eaten rocks. But then, as Silas opened her door and offered her his hand, that bubbling warmth filled her right up again.

They walked to the front, which was even prettier than she remembered, hands intertwined like it was the most natural thing for them. And the crazy thing was that it *did* feel natural. Like she was right where she was always supposed to be, with her fingers laced through his.

He paid happily at the gate and, just like that, they were in.

And it was *lovely.* So bright, richer and lusher than her memory could ever hope to recall. It stretched out in an impressive way, and she was incredibly glad she'd worn comfortable shoes. She wanted to see all of it, read every display, soak up every bit of knowledge that she could until her brain was bursting.

Goodness knew her heart already felt like doing so.

"I think," Silas said beside her, voice so quiet she almost didn't catch it. "That if I could keep you as happy as you are now in this moment, I could die a satisfied man."

Oh, if *that* didn't just make her heart thunder in her chest.

"I feel like I should say something witty," she said, "but I'm tapped out. You'll have to come again later if you want my acerbic wit."

He squeezed her hand, his long fingers big enough to cover most of the back of her palm. "That's alright. You stay this way as long as you like."

"You'll regret you said that when we're stuck in here until closing time, and I'm rattling off the Latin names of everything I might be able to grow."

"No," he said with a grin. "I don't think I would regret that at all."

Now that wasn't fair at all! Feeling like she was already bubbling to bursting, she tugged on his hand and pulled him forward.

It was like they walked into a magical world, just the two of them, all the other guests fading away. It was everything that she had ever dreamed of and more, making her wonder why she'd never taken herself. She had enough money for admission, and she was pretty much always guaranteed a car, so why did it take some charming man in cowboy boots to remind her that sometimes she needed to do things just for fun too?

Funny, he said that she had opened his eyes, but she felt like he was the one who had done that to her, reminding her that she couldn't always just keep going and going and going and going. She loved her community, yes, and she loved the shop, but she needed more than that to be healthy. Hadn't Andre been trying to get her to get a hobby that was just for her?

It was about two hours later when they reached one of the koi ponds, complete with a beautiful pagoda in the middle of a bridge and dozens of wisterias and weeping willows.

"Oh! The koi!" she cried, rushing forward. "The fishies!"

Despite being a twenty-four-year-old woman, she ran right up to the edge and looked down. Most of the koi were by the bridge, but there were a few of them swimming around lazily, the sun glinting off their beautiful sides.

"Oh man," she said, following along until she was on the bridge and kneeling down. "I love these little guys."

"Really?" Silas asked, sounding surprised. "Is there something special about them?"

Teddy shrugged. "I dunno. They're big, pretty fish with kinda cute faces. They look real personable, you know?"

He laughed, and his expression wasn't mocking, just gently amused. "If you say so."

"I do say so. Ooooh, they used to have these things you can put a quarter into that spits out food for them. I wonder if they're still around?"

"I think I see one on the opposite end of the bridge, judging by the line of people waiting patiently."

"That's definitely it. You have any change? I'm gonna get *so* much of the kibble."

Another laugh, and it was still just as lovely a sound as it had always been. "How about you stay here and say 'hi' to all your fish friends, and I'll go stand in line for you?"

"I mean, if you're offering."

"I am."

He headed off and Teddy leaned down to look at the fish.

They were so used to being fed fat and silly that even her shadow was enough to bring them curiously up to the top of their water, their mouths gaping at her as if to demand the treats immediately.

But then she caught her reflection on the water, distorted and rippling, making her face look nearly malformed. It was just a flash, but it was enough to have all those insecurities come creeping right back up on her.

He was rich. He was out of her league. He would get bored with her. He would realize that she wasn't feminine or graceful or any of those good things that he and his family probably valued. She was too low class, too dirty. They probably wanted some pristine church girl, a real virginal maiden type who was content to cook and clean and pop out babies. Teddy didn't even want to *think* about babies until she was twenty-eight. At the earliest.

A shadow appeared beside her, darkening more of the water, and Teddy turned, expecting Silas. But instead, it was an older lady dressed like someone might if they were going to church.

"I hope you don't mind me saying, but you look like you're thinking some heavy thoughts."

Teddy had no idea who the grandma was, but there was something welcoming about her. Or maybe she was so desperate to get her thoughts out of her head that she was willing to trust a complete stranger.

"I do?" Teddy said.

"A penny for your thoughts?"

No, that was ridiculous. She wasn't going to spill her guts to some little old lady just because she seemed likable. That would be utterly—

"I like a guy," Teddy blurted out.

"Is that so? I happen to like many people."

"I mean, I like a guy a *lot*. I think that one day, it'd be pretty easy to fall in love with him."

"Oh, I see. I remember that excitement. The rush. But you seem more stressed than any of those other lovely things."

"I suppose because I am."

The woman made an affirmative sound, and Teddy found herself rattling off again. "The thing is, it's just been me and my family for so long. My whole world has been my garden, the community, and the shop.

"This guy I like? He's so outside of all those things that he's practically on another planet. And I guess that's kinda terrifying. And I wonder if that makes me a coward, and it also makes me wonder if I'm just setting myself up to be hurt later. My mom trusted the wrong person, and even though she got me, she carried those scars with her until the day she died."

"I see."

Teddy waited for her to continue; she could feel that something else was coming on.

The grandma started talking again, "You are a strong woman, that much is clear. But have you considered that, potentially, you don't always have to *be* strong?"

"What do you mean?"

"Well, to be strong, you must be rigid. Protected. You spend all this time building up a great and terrible armor around yourself that it's easy to forget there was ever another way of being. And the thought of being out there, without your armor, of having someone seeing you all vulnerable and *weak*? Well, that sounds terrifying to me."

Teddy let out a heavy breath and looked over her shoulder at the woman. "You do this often?"

"Pardon?"

The wizened wrinkles of her face caught the light, making her look somewhat alien and powerful, but her eyes were kind. She reminded Teddy of some of the grammies that were at her own church. "Impart wisdom to random people at ponds?"

She let out a gentle, lilting laugh. "The pond is unusual, but you wouldn't be the first young woman in distress that I've helped."

"So it is a habit then?"

The smile across her face was ageless but, at the same time, spoke of a rich history that Teddy could only guess at. "Kindness should always be a habit. As with empathy."

Teddy nodded, looking back to the fish. "So you think I'm being a coward then?"

"Goodness no. Being scared doesn't make you a coward. Do you think David didn't feel fear when he looked up at that giant who had killed hundreds of his kin? That Joshua wasn't ever scared? Fear is natural. You can let it control you or choose to defy it." Her words washed over Teddy, and the mechanic tried to open herself up to the ideas the woman was presenting.

"Of course, there's this myth that if the stakes are great enough, that fear shouldn't matter. But these matters of the heart aren't quite like that, are they? I think you'll have to decide for you, and only for you. Not anybody else."

"That's easier said than done," Teddy murmured to the fish.

"Nothing I've said is easy. If it were, I think more people would be much happier." She let out a pleasant little sort of hum, and then she was pressing something into Teddy's hand. "My granddaughter will be coming for me soon, I think. Here, you take these."

With that she tottered off, like some sort of strange, advice-vending elder. When Teddy looked down into her palm, there was about a half-portion of koi-kibble in it.

"Huh, let my walls down?"

After everything they'd gone through since they'd met, she would have thought it would be easy. But if the random grandma said it wasn't supposed to be easy at all, maybe it made sense why Teddy was having trouble.

Maybe she needed time, and bit by bit she could open up. And maybe the thought of being open and honest and vulnerable with Silas wouldn't make her so nauseous. She could adjust to not having the shield of debt between them as an excuse not to deal with her feelings.

"You look like you're in deep thought."

This time it was Silas who approached her, and she sent him an uncertain smile. "Would you believe you're not the first person to tell me that today?"

"Oh? Were the fish getting mouthy with you while I was gone?"

"Hah, no. Nothing like that. Just a lot on my mind." She took the kibble from him and scattered some across the water. Soon the pond was lit up by flashes of gold, onyx, white and orange. It was soothing, in a way, and a beautiful sight to behold. "Thinking about the future."

"It's pretty scary, isn't it?" Silas said, completely unaware of the churning thoughts in front of her.

"You know I'm not like a lot of women, right?" she blurted, the grandma's words playing in her head. "Not like a lot of people, I guess?"

Silas's grin slowly slid from his face. "What do you mean?"

"I mean," she swallowed. "I just mean that I'm different. I'm... intense. I can be a bit withheld sometimes. It's hard for me to trust people, and sometimes my brain tells me that people are up to the worst things. It took me close to a year to finally get that Andre wasn't going to chase me out when he grew tired of me, and a good year and a half after that to make my first connections in the neighborhood.

"Once I get there, I'm one of the most loyal people. I'd lay down my life for anyone in our community. It just... it just..." She closed her eyes, so many thoughts flying through her head. Her father. Her mother. Cruel folks at school. Amazing people at school. Warm hugs from Mr. Abadi. Kisses on the cheek from Mrs. Routier. Antonio's warm eyes as he laughed. Snide comments about her skin, about her father. All of it was mixed up and complicated, with the worst coming from outside of her home and everything good coming from within.

But Silas was good. She was almost certain of that. And he was from the outside. That had to mean something.

"It's so hard for me to trust people," she said and let loose a sigh.

She was surprised when Silas plopped down right beside her, crossing his legs so they didn't go into the water.

"Teddy, I'm twenty-eight years old and I've only ever dated two people in my whole life. I thought it was just because I didn't mesh. That people weren't for me. Not a good fit, you know?

"So maybe you are different from everybody else. But maybe I am too. The only thing that really matters to me is that my different seems to gel pretty nicely with your different. And if this doesn't go right? If we go on a few dates and you decide this isn't for you, then I'll have an amazing friend."

Teddy licked her lips, her heart beating fast. "But what if you decide that it's not for you?"

He smiled that charming, roguish smile that she'd noticed from day one. "Well, that's not an issue. I already know how I feel. But I don't mind if you need time to figure out how you do."

She fed the fish more kibble. "You're too nice to me, you know that?"

"Actually, I think I'm not nearly as nice as you deserve. But if you like, we can debate about it while we continue to walk around."

Teddy's spirits lifted, and she was quickly returning to those warm thoughts. She wasn't going to fix everything in her head that day. She wasn't going to magically stop being scared. But maybe, if she allowed herself to, she could begin the first steps toward being a more happy, whole person.

"I'd like that quite a bit."

23

———

Silas

S ilas glanced over to where Teddy was sitting, her head leaning against the car window as she looked out at the lights whipping by. They had walked and walked around that garden until her feet had ached, and they still hadn't gotten through the whole place. He'd like to take her again, if they got a chance.

He could tell that something had been bothering her when they'd first arrived at the gardens, and for a good hour or so, he had been so sure that she wasn't into him, that she felt pressured into the date. But then she had spoken to him at the pond about what was troubling her, and suddenly everything made sense.

Silas was well aware that there were probably certain expectations about his taste. That he might like a waifish, modelesque woman like so many of the socialites he knew. Or maybe even a submissive, soft-spoken church debutante.

But no, he had eyes only for a certain curvaceous mechanic with flaming red hair and poliosis—which had nothing to do with what FDR had. He had something for a woman who has carried the weight of the world on her shoulders for so long that she's forgotten what it's like to share the burden. He had a thing for her button nose, for the faint freckles across her cheeks. He had a thing for the baleful way she would stare at a piece of equipment when it was giving her trouble. He had a thing for the way she looked with a baseball bat, defending her turf.

Silas had never really believed in destiny, but as he looked over at Teddy, he couldn't help but feel like God couldn't have made a better match for him. Or maybe he was the one who was the match for her. A match for each other? Yeah, that was it.

"I can feel you staring at me, you know?" she murmured, her eyes remaining closed.

"I assure you; I'm looking at the road. I'm a very responsible driver."

"Oh yeah? Then why are the hairs on the back of my neck standing on end?"

"My electrifying personality?"

A chuckle sounded from her and she sat up, opening her eyes. "Wow, I'm glad our date's over if that's the humor I have to look forward to."

"Ouch. I'm insulted."

"Well, it certainly wasn't meant as a compliment."

Then they were laughing together. Silas felt like he could name on one hand the people who spoke to him so frankly, who were willing to banter with him and go toe to toe. And all of those people were his brothers. "Good to know that I'll always have you around to cut down my ego."

"Of course. Consider it a community service. On the house."

"Your generosity knows no bounds."

"Oh, it's got bounds, alright. I'm just still figuring them out."

That sounded important. "Oh?"

She didn't answer right away, but he had learned that he needed to be still and wait for her to figure out exactly what she wanted to say. That was one of the things he always appreciated about Teddy; she didn't kowtow or capitulate. What she said was always what she meant.

"I got to talking with this older lady today, and I guess I realized a few things."

"Good things?"

"Not sure yet. But important things. And one of them is, in order to open up, I need to set some boundaries."

Silas felt his brows furrow. "I don't think I follow."

"I didn't realize it, but I've kinda built my entire life to be about what I do for others. If I was productive enough, or helpful enough, I felt like I was worthy of their love. And don't get me wrong, there's nothing wrong with helping and taking care of those around me, but instead of doing it out of love, or happiness, I was doing it in some sort of desperate bid to force them to love me."

"But you don't need to make anyone love you, Teddy."

"I think I'm starting to realize that. That I don't have to pay back any of them, because there's nothing owed. I may have come here an orphan with a lot of anger, but I'm not that anymore. I don't have to keep trying to make up for my past mistakes."

"I'm glad to hear that." He would hate it if she felt obligated to pay back his kindness. That was the opposite of what he wanted.

"Thanks. But if I'm going to get better at all that stuff, I'm gonna have to set boundaries for myself. Cut myself off when I get real insecure, or people-pleasey."

"Don't worry. I'll warn you the moment you get too agreeable. We can't have that."

Thankfully she laughed and seemed to relax. Or she did until she realized he was pulling up to her family's shop.

"Oh, are we here already? It feels like we just left the gardens."

He smiled, appreciating the slight disappointment to her tone. She wanted things to keep going. Despite all his worry, she seemed to have enjoyed herself. "You were dozing there for a while."

"Really? Man, I hope I didn't snore."

"Is *that* what that was?" he joked, unbuckling his seat belt and getting out. "I thought my engine needed to be serviced."

She elbowed him before he could slip out of reach and cross around the front of the vehicle. "*Rude.* Just for that, next time I cook, I'm over-salting your food."

"I'm not so sure that you would be able to live with yourself if you ruined a perfectly good meal."

"You never know. I'm working on opening myself, aren't I?"

He held out his hand to her, helping her out of his car. "I think that might be pushing the idea a bit far."

She laughed at that, and he felt himself puff up in pride. He loved that sound and the way that her eyes would light up, her head tilting back slightly. She was a vision, always, but she always looked best when she was happy.

What would it be like if he could keep her that way? All

pink-cheeked and contented. Was it even possible? To be her shoulder to lean on, her entertainment during the lows in life, her comforter during the worst times? He was probably getting much too far ahead of himself, but he could scold himself later. For the moment he just wanted to watch her as she shared her mirth with him.

"Alright, fair enough. I suppose there's a limit to growth."

"Not sure poisoning my food via over-salination is growth, but I'm glad you agree."

"Yeah, yeah, don't get used to it."

"I wouldn't dream of it."

They reached her door far too quickly, and disappointment bloomed inside of him. He didn't want to let her go. He wanted to hold her there in that moment, away from all the troubles and stresses that came with their lives.

"Well," she said, turning to face him, her back against the door. He couldn't help but notice that she didn't let go of his hand, tethering him to her like she didn't want him to go either. "I realize this is where I should leave you, but it's not wise to stand outside for goodbyes. Even if you did fix my little wanna-be-gangster problem for the moment."

"You want me to come in?" he asked, his mouth going dry.

Gosh, she looked like a dream, head tilted up to him, eyes wide and uncertain. She was shining gold, bathed in the yellow glow of the streetlights, her red hair done up in a bun and her eyes lined in that pin-up style of hers. She was something out of a museum or an exhibition. And she was looking at him like she saw something important inside of him too.

"Just into the reception area," she said softly. "You know, for a proper goodbye."

"Yeah, we wouldn't want to be improper." Did his voice

sound raspy or was it just him? He didn't know, and he certainly wasn't going to ask.

Teddy pulled her hand from him, turning to the door and unlocking it. She stepped in, pulling him behind her, then closed the door.

She didn't turn the lights on, however, the only illumination coming from outside. It made everything look magical, a bit more surreal. And this time, when she turned around quickly, he knew it was purposeful when they ended up less than a breath away from each other.

"I want to thank you for a really lovely time," she murmured, that look on her face again. The one that made his heart race and wonder if maybe he was imagining everything because it all seemed too good to be true.

"I'm glad you enjoyed yourself. Maybe, if you're not too busy, we can do it again soon."

"Well, I'll have you know that I'm no longer regularly running off to work at this manor that's an hour and a half away, so my schedule is a lot more open than it used to be."

"Is that so?" he asked, feeling his bravery pick up right along with his heart rate. Although one of his hands was holding hers, the other was free to do what it wanted, so he brought his arm up, wrapping it around her waist and pulling her flush to him.

It was the most they had ever touched, not merely brushing against each other, but pressing into each other with intent. She was so warm against his arm, and her front melted to his just as he had imagined. Even her smell was lovely, warm and smelling of the flowers they had spent all day around. It was perfect.

"Last I knew, it was," she answered breathily, her free hand coming up to rest on his shoulder. Her fingers gently brushed against his collar, tracing the weave of the cloth and making goosebumps rise along his flesh.

He felt like time was going impossibly slow but racing at the same time. Every single detail of what was happening rushed him at once, a cacophony of importance. He wanted to hang onto all of it, never forgetting a single thing.

"Well then, it's a date," he said.

"Don't you think we should finish up our first one?"

"Maybe." He felt his head tilting downward, drawn ever closer to those plush lips of hers. "But I wouldn't mind staying like this for a while."

She swallowed, and he watched that alluring bob of her throat again. The rest of the world was falling away, leaving just the two of them, and the electricity that sparked along everywhere they touched. "It *is* pretty nice."

"Isn't it?"

She nodded, then tucked her face into his chest. He could feel her breath rasping across his front, warm and speedy. At least she seemed to be almost as affected as he was.

But at the same time, that didn't seem quite possible, because he felt like he was ramping up to some sort of inexplicable rush. Something important and maybe a little dangerous or maybe something that was exactly perfect.

Teddy spoke next. "This weekend, would you help me make my deliveries, and then you can meet my mom?"

"Your mother?" He must have misheard her, her voice muffled by his chest. He had never heard Teddy talk about her mom, and he had assumed she was out of the picture. If her mother was around, then why was she living with Andre? "Where does she live?"

"She doesn't." She pulled her face away from his chest and gave him a wan smile at his clear confusion. "She's buried at the old church, but I still visit her when I can. I'd like you to meet her."

"Oh..." There was so much he still needed to learn about her. Her mother was dead? What had happened? No wonder she was so dedicated to family. No one cherished those around them more than those who had lost everything. So yeah, maybe she had some hang-ups about that, but suddenly they made a lot more sense.

"But we don't have to if you think that's creepy," she said quickly, and he realized that she had misinterpreted his tone.

"No, I would love to. I'm honored that you trust me with something like that."

"Yeah, well, I'm trying this new thing out where I take some select folks at their face value instead of assuming they're out to get my family and me."

"...select folks is just me, isn't it?"

One of her fingers flicked against his chin before resting back on his shoulder. "Hey, we all gotta start somewhere."

He knew his smile was absolutely dorkish in response, but he didn't care. "Well, I'm certainly not complaining."

"Good, because I'd hate to kick you out right now. I'm rather enjoying the moment."

"Me too."

Her fingers continued exploring, gently stroking. Eventually, however, they reached an area he wasn't used to people touching, one he hid from everyone.

"What's this raised area?" Teddy asked, her voice low. Contented.

He was sure that he could tell her it was nothing; he was even tempted to. But if he wanted Teddy to trust him, didn't he need to do the same for her?

"It's my scar."

"Scar?"

He nodded, not quite looking down at her. Afraid that of what he might see. "Yeah."

"You mentioned it before, I think. That time I caught you after the gym."

"Yeah. So, you've seen it." He'd almost forgotten about that moment, how exposed he had felt. But as he recalled it, the last thing he expected was a chuckle from her.

"I don't know how to tell you this, but I was a little distracted by, well, all you got going on. I didn't notice any scar."

"What?"

She tilted her head up so just the point of her chin was resting on his chest. "I said, you're too hot for your own good and all those shining muscles dazzled me. I didn't notice a scar."

How could she not notice his scar? It was ugly and raised. *Awful.* He hated it more than anything else.

"You're just saying that to make me feel better."

Now she leaned back fully, giving him a solid *look*. The same kind he'd seen Frenchie give Solomon once or twice. "When have I ever said something that I didn't mean?"

Okay. That was fair. "Sorry," he apologized with a breath. "I just find it hard to believe."

She shrugged, and the small movement made him acutely aware of how close they were to each other. "What happened?"

"It was a childish accident. My brothers and I were playing with fireworks that we had no right to be around when we were kids. I happened to be the unlucky one who got hurt. I threw this firecracker in the air, but something must have been wrong with the fuse or the mix because it exploded right in front of me. Burned me from my right collarbone down to my first ribs. I got some skin grafts for some parts of it, but I still ended up with some nasty scars toward the top."

"Oh."

She went quiet again, and for a moment he thought she was going to drop it. That didn't seem to be the case, however, because then she was speaking again. "Can I touch it?"

"What?" Surely, he misheard her. She couldn't have said that.

"Can I touch it?"

No! Of course not! Why would someone so beautiful, so soft and perfect, want to touch his ugly old scar? It was a testament to his stupidity. To recklessness. He'd learned a lot that day, and he bore the reminder with plenty of chagrin. Maybe that was why he wasn't as cocky as his brother, Sterling, but he wasn't sure the outcome was worth the price.

"You don't have to let me if you're not comfortable," she said.

Oh.

But the way she said it, the way she *looked* at him, and he felt himself wanting to agree. Teddy was one of the kindest people he knew. If he could trust anyone with a twisted part of him, it was her.

Trust.

They kept coming back to that. Over and over. It almost felt like God was trying to teach him something but was doing so by swatting him repeatedly with a newspaper.

"No," he said finally. "It's alright."

He let go of her hand, undoing about half of the buttons on the shirt he'd picked especially for the date. It was a light blue, and his mom said it looked lovely with his darker features, the features that he'd gotten from her. Each button made the fear rise in him a little more, as well as the certainty that this was going to be the straw that pushed Teddy away in revulsion.

It seemed an age until his white undershirt peeked out from underneath his top layer, along with his old cross necklace. He couldn't go any farther, afraid his hands might start shaking and reveal how scared he was, so he let them drop to his sides. That didn't seem to matter, however, because soon her fingers were in the gap, pulling back the fabric until the area was revealed.

She couldn't see all of it, not with his undershirt there, and so those same fingers tugged gently at the collar of it, easing it down until she could see the jagged, biting edges of the wound.

"It looks like lightning," she said, her tone almost reverent.

And then one of those fingers *touched* it.

It was an inexplicable sensation, her living digit against his dead flesh. But she didn't poke, she didn't prod, and when he looked down, he saw that she was gently tracing it. Like a map. Not like a hideous, bubbled, twisted thing.

"Like lightning?" he asked, swallowing hard. Why wasn't she shuddering? Why wasn't she pitying him?

"Yeah, like lightning." Her finger continued moving, feeling the bumps of it. The pits. The artificial and stitch-whipped lines where the skin grafts hadn't taken and where they bled into his uninjured flesh. An eternity passed as she mapped him out, him standing there in his stupor, watching as the most beautiful woman he'd ever met caressed the most hideous parts of him.

When she finished, he felt shaky. Like reality was crumbly at the edges and he'd just imagined something that couldn't be true. He'd been aware that he was a relatively handsome guy ever since he finished puberty, but there was a line of what a handsome face could get people to look past, and his scar was it. And yet... it didn't even seem like a line at all to Teddy. Which didn't make any sense. People like him were supposed to be flawless on the outside, like all his brothers.

"Why do you hide this part of you?" she asked gently.

He blinked at her, trying to catch up. She had to know. Surely, she was teasing him. "Because it's ugly," he answered as if it were a matter of fact. Because it was a matter of fact. He'd been told by people at school, seen kids pointing at water parks when he was younger. Even his doctor had commented that it was a doozy of a scar.

"I don't think so," she said, just as plainly. "It's a story. It's a marker of something you survived. Something you beat. It's like my hair."

"Your hair?"

She nodded, smiling softly at him. That sort of smile that dug into the dark thoughts of his and shoved them back. "Yeah. Some people tell me that I should dye it. That it's tacky, or that people get the wrong impression, but I like it."

"You like it." He wasn't sure when he had turned into a parrot, but his brain was hard rebooting, and all that he could do was copy her while it tried to catch up.

"Yeah. It's a scar, sure. An injury to my body that came from me doing something real dumb, but it's *me*. It's my life. It's a reminder of a lesson I learned, along with a whole bunch of memories of how my mom cared for me after that. I'll never forget her holding my hand the entire time we were in the emergency room, or how she would clean and change my bandages at home, a worried expression on her face.

"Yeah, it hurt like a whip at the time, but after long enough, all that pain is gone and what I have left is the story and all the nice things." Carefully, she buttoned him back up, gentle and tender as ever. Once he was covered up, she leaned forward to press the tiniest of pecks to his collarbone, right where the reddest, most taught part of it was. "Not to trivialize things, but I think your scar is pretty cool."

He let out a long breath that he didn't even know he was holding. "Cool, huh?"

She sent him a mischievous look before her face was buried right back in his chest. He knew that her cheek had to feel the bottom part of the raised scar, but she didn't care.

She was incredible.

"One might even say hot," Teddy said.

He couldn't help but grin at that. "As long as they don't say it around my mom."

"I'll remember to be on my best behavior then. Assuming I ever meet her."

Goodness, he desperately hoped things worked out enough where they would meet. He could only imagine the gardening paradise the two would build with each other.

And just like that, the rising panic in him, the nausea, all of it was gone. She didn't care about his scar. She thought it was *cool*. A testament to his life. He wasn't magically alright with it, but maybe if he tried to look at the raised mass of skin, he could see it like she did.

He supposed he owed it to her to at least try. Silently, he told himself he would do just that, and the pair slipped into a comfortable quiet.

They kept holding each other, in each other's spheres longer than they had ever been before. With all of his worry and disgust about his scar out of the way for the moment, all that was left within him was a strange mix of feeling like he was amped for a fight but also perfectly content. His heart was hammering in his chest, thumping away steadily like the engines that Teddy spent so much time working on, but it wasn't unpleasant. In fact, he would be content to feel so elated all the time.

Except he still wanted... *more.*

"Teddy?" he whispered, telling himself to shut up, but the words were coming out anyway.

"Hmmm?" she murmured, and he felt the vibrations against his chest.

"I would very much like to kiss you now."

There, he said it. Come what may, if he was asking her to trust him and be vulnerable, the least he could do was be honest with her.

And he *did* want to kiss her. Desperately. He'd thought about her lips probably much more often than was polite, and all of it felt like it was reaching a boiling point. She was so beautiful, so kind. Was it wrong for him to want to show affection for her in the way that was always lauded by every romantic work?

She pulled away from his chest again, both of her cheeks red as she looked up at him with half-lidded eyes. "I was hoping you'd do something like that."

His heart jumped, somewhere between shocked and ecstatic. She wanted him, or at least wanted to *try.* And that was all he could ask for, all things considered. More than he deserved.

The dam of reserve within him cracked, and then he was bending down to crash his lips against hers, Teddy going onto her tiptoes at the same time. They met in a clash that probably should have been sloppy, should have been full of clicking teeth and discomfort, but instead it was everything he could have ever wanted and more.

They let go of each other's hands, if only so that her arms

could wrap around his neck, pulling him down to her, and his arms could encircle her soft, generous middle.

He could hear her breath quicken as their mouths moved against each other. It thrilled Silas to know that she was just as affected by it as he was. He wasn't alone in his insanity for her, in the rush, the excitement of it all.

Everything she was giving him was borderline intoxicating, and he wanted to show her that he was grateful for every ounce of it. He knew he didn't deserve her, that he'd spent almost thirty years of his life doing not much besides helping his dad hurt people like her. But she *forgave* him. And although she didn't fully trust him yet, she *wanted* to. It was more than he could ever ask for, ever expect, and yet that was exactly what she was giving him.

Boundaries, his conscience reminded him.

With a ragged breath, he broke the kiss, taking the scantest of steps back as his chest heaved.

"What's wrong?" Teddy asked, looking up at him with a hazy gaze, her face flushed and lips puffy from his affection.

"Speaking of trust, I think that's as far as I trust myself right about now."

Teddy regarded him curiously, not seeming to understand.

Clearing his throat, Silas searched for words. He had a lot of them—usually—but at the moment he was doing a terrible job of remembering any of them. "I might have wandered in college. Made some mistakes and decisions that I wish I could take back now. But one thing I learned is that there are certain parts of a relationship I don't want to rush into. Certain things that should be cherished. Waited for."

He knew he sounded old-fashioned, but it was true for him. When he'd first stumbled, it had been with a girl that he thought he would be with for life. But then she had turned out not to be who she said at all, and when things had fallen apart, he was left feeling like he had given a chunk of himself to the wrong person.

"Are you telling me that you want to wait?" Teddy said, sounding surprised.

He supposed it was an odd thing in a man of his age, but maybe that was another reason why he'd never dated after college. Too much was expected that he wasn't comfortable giving to just anybody.

"Yes. I would very much like that," he said.

She had an odd expression on her face, one that made him feel self-conscious despite how high the kiss had sent him flying.

"What is it?" he asked.

"Nothing," she answered quickly, and the answer hung heavy between them. But then she was sighing and speaking again. "I guess I'm used to guys chasing my body more than... other parts of me," she said finally. "The same sort of thing happened to my mom."

More about her mother. He really did have so much to learn about her, and he was excited about every single crumb she would bequeath to him. But that could come later; first there was the moment they were in and the unwelcome uncertainty in her eyes.

He cupped that wonderful, beautiful face of hers.

"I assure you, from the bottom of my heart, that I am interested in more than just your body." He leaned forward, having the will power to gently press the softest kiss to the tip of her nose before pulling back. "I would be lying if I said I wasn't attracted to you. If I tried to deny that kissing you doesn't make me want to maybe... rush things, but you deserve more than that. I want to *know* you, Teddy. All of you.

Your mind, your body and your soul. That's what's important to me."

She let out a laugh that sounded almost like a sob, winded and open. Raw. It made him want to wrap his arms around her and hold her forever, protect her from all those memories that made such a terrible sound come out of her.

"I don't think that anybody's ever said that to me before."

"That's a sin if I ever heard one," Silas murmured. "But I'll be happy to say it over and over again until you're sick of it."

"I don't think I'd ever get sick of it."

"Then I'll keep on saying it forever."

Another ragged sound came out of her, and when her eyes flicked back to his, they were damp with unshed tears. "Can I have one more kiss? A small one? Then it'll be goodnight."

"Of course." He would hold himself back for her. She deserved respect. She deserved the effort. The idea that no one had been willing to wait for her, that she felt valued as an object rather than a whole person, helped cool his desire that had been burning unchecked. No matter how much his body wanted her, he wanted what was best for her first and foremost. "A kiss goodnight, just for you."

"Just for me," she whispered, and then their lips were molding together once again.

It was different than the first one. Gentle, slow. More vulnerable when the urgent desires were taken out. But it made his heart ache in all the right ways. Made him *hurt* for her in a way that he never wanted to stop.

And when they broke the kiss, the look she gave him was worth every ounce of restraint.

"See you this weekend," she said, taking a step back.

"See you this weekend," he confirmed before turning toward the door. It did take a great deal of effort, but he managed to get himself all the way out and onto the street before he looked back over his shoulder. There he saw Teddy closing the door, but not before she sent him out one adorable little wave. If the men of her shop saw her, they would probably never let her live it down, and he promised himself he'd never forget it either.

But then the door was closed, and it was time for him to get in the car. He had a whole hour plus to think about what had happened—to replay every minute detail until it was burned into his memory like a scar.

And that was a scar he would have no problem cherishing.

EPILOGUE

Theodora

Eighteen months later

Somehow, a whole year and a half had passed in the blink of an eye.

Teddy didn't know what happened. One minute she was just starting to date the middle son of a ranching empire; the next she was helping to host a massive dinner and children's play at the community center that the Miller family had sponsored.

So much had happened in between, seemingly a lifetime's worth, and yet it'd all been accomplished in eighteen short months.

First of all, Teddy did end up meeting all of Silas' family. Not all at once, thank goodness, but even broken up it was always a somewhat overwhelming experience. His mom was lovely, and they ended up getting on as thick as thieves. It turned out Mrs. McLintoc Miller loved anyone who knew which plants were beneficially cohabitable with others and proper timing for planting different seedlings. The two of them had plans for making a very impressive community garden together in a vacant lot on the very south edge of the neighborhood, where they could help their own area but also their neighboring one as well.

As for Silas' dad… she could tell that he wasn't overly fond of Frenchie *or* her. He always managed to not be around when they were over at the manor. But that was okay with Teddy. Solomon and Silas were supportive of her and Frenchie and never made her feel inadequate.

She'd met Samuel once when he came down with his lovely fiancé for Simon's graduation party. Now she talked with Virginia fairly regularly, even if it was only to send memes and jokes about fighting to each other. She was one of the only women Teddy had ever met who liked to throw down as much as she did.

Of course, Virginia kept insisting that she needed to meet someone named Missy, who apparently was just as much of a brawler as them, but Teddy hadn't managed to get the free time to go up and visit Silas' extended family.

"Hey, Teddy, everything's handled. Why don't you come and sit down for a minute?"

She looked up to see Jamani, all dressed up for her role in the show. Teddy had had a feeling that the girl would be perfect for the after-school drama program that Mrs. Sanchez had started as soon as the community center was up and open, and it turned out she was right.

"I just have—"

The young woman cleared her throat and crossed her arms, looking every bit of the rising star that she was. "*Teddy.* You sit. Now."

It was hard not to chuckle, so Teddy put her hands up in surrender instead. "Since when do you get to talk to me like an adult?"

"Since I turned thirteen. I *am* an adult."

"Right, because that's definitely the marker we're going by now." She gave another hard look, and Teddy finally surrendered entirely. "Alright, alright. I give in. Lead me away to my prison—I mean, my seat."

Jamani rolled her eyes but seemed all too happy to march Teddy out. It didn't take long for her to lead Teddy to a table, as Sterling, Mrs. Miller, Andre, and Roman were all there. Solomon and Frenchie had wanted to come, but they were off helping one of her friends who had gotten into a spot of trouble in another state. Teddy didn't mind. She knew Solomon and Frenchie supported her entirely.

Sterling had taken longer to come around.

He was a nice person, in general. And funny too. But it was clear that his sibling rivalry streak with his twin had grown stronger as Silas pulled away from the mold his dad tried to force them all into. Teddy kept hoping that he would realize he could forge his own path and grow. One time, when he'd made a crack about Silas' scar, she'd drawn a strong line and chewed him out so hard he had avoided her for a month.

He was better now. He respected her boundaries and tried to be a good friend to the both of them.

"Oh goodness," Mrs. Miller said as she sat. "I am so looking forward to this. Thank you for inviting me, Theodora."

That was one thing Teddy could never convince the woman to do; call her by her nickname. But still, she didn't mind the older woman using her full name. It was delightfully old-fashioned in a way. And although the woman still sometimes struggled with the paths her sons were taking, or with understanding certain lifestyles that were foreign from her own, Teddy would always appreciate that she at least *tried*.

"I didn't know you had an appreciation for the arts," Sterling said, leaning over to kiss his mom's gray hair.

"That's because I ended up with sons who all liked to play football, lacrosse, or swim. I had hoped that one of you might be like your middle cousin and have more artistic ability, but I suppose y'all came out alright."

Her eyes twinkled mischievously at that, and Sterling sputtered in mock offense. "Just alright though. Don't butter me up too much, Mom."

"If you're really so worried about it, maybe one of you could finally get married and give me some grandchildren to dote on, and I won't have to rely on lovely community productions."

Roman nearly choked on his water, and Andre laughed outright. He was supposed to have a date for the night, but unfortunately the flu had her bedridden as of two days earlier.

That was one of the things she was happiest about. After a *lot* of gentle persistence, Jamal had gotten his wish and Andre had agreed to a single date with his mother. Well, one date turned into two, two turned into four, and four turned into a weekly habit. They were taking it slow; they'd both been through so much, but it made Teddy's heart glow to see Andre happy again. In love. She was pretty sure that he had given up on ever having a life outside of his children and the shop, and she couldn't be more grateful that he'd found the motivation to try again.

As for Roman, he wasn't dating anyone as far as she knew,

but he was taking online business classes. The shop was doing so well that he was talking about looking into a secondary location. Maybe even branding. It was all above Teddy's head considering everything she had on her plate, but it was so wonderful seeing her brother have dreams. Ambitions. Something to talk about excitedly at the dinner table each night.

Because they still ate dinner together. They were still a family. They weren't any lesser for having found more to their lives than just each other. If anything, they were *more*. And healthier. Definitely happier.

"Where's Silas?" she asked, looking around. She'd seen him arrive, but she was so busy laying out the snacks, drinks and making sure there was appropriate signage on how to find the bathroom that she hadn't seen him beyond that.

"He's helping with the performance," Mrs. Miller said, pride written plainly across her features. "Apparently the lighting guy had some sort of hand injury, I think it was? So he needed someone to handle, I'm not sure I got this part right. The ropes?"

That made sense. "Wow, I hope Dymtro is alright. I didn't know he was hurt."

"He should be fine, probably just a little tender." The lights began to dim, and the older woman sucked in an excited breath. "Oh, it's starting!"

A quiet fell over the twenty-odd tables in the room. Technically the wide, open space they were in was a gymnasium, but it had been built with the idea of having multiple uses. Which was why there was a stage inset into one wall, complete with a beautiful cobalt curtain and all the sound equipment they could ever need.

The Millers really had gone above and beyond, even if their patriarch didn't seem to get it. Her whole neighborhood had a place for intermural sports teams, community productions, holiday dinners, events, and an emergency shelter in case of disasters. It was a boon to them, a way to enrich the lives of the entire town and would continue to do so for generations. She wasn't sure Silas even understood just how much he had added to everyone's lives, but hey, she could spend the whole rest of the year reminding him.

Or maybe the production would do a better job of it, because the youngest kids were marching on, dressed up like robots in costumes that Teddy knew were made of meticulously painted cardboard boxes courtesy of Mr. Abadi. Turned out the older man had been an artist back in the day and, although he couldn't assemble them himself, he certainly could decorate them. They did a very short but adorable number about building blocks and being a team. Teddy wasn't sure she quite got it, never having a younger sibling herself and being blissfully out of the loop when it came to young people entertainment, but it was enjoyable nonetheless.

After the young ones, it was the older kids, the ones just about to hit their teen years. They were all different kinds of animals, some costumes more elaborate than others based on what Mrs. Sanchez could scrounge/make. Although the new community drama program had a grant—courtesy of the Millers—she and the other heads were still relatively frugal. Teddy didn't blame them.

The animals didn't really have a dance, but rather told a parable about all the animals and who was the mightiest of them all. Jamani was in that one, and she ended up being the mouse that was declared the king over all the others, having won all their tests. She rocked the roll, of course. But Teddy had never doubted that she would. The whole thing was cheesy, naturally, but that made it perfect, and everyone applauded when they took their bows.

The teens after them were different. There was a young girl that sang, her voice high and lilting, angelic as it washed over them. Teddy closed her eyes and listened, feeling her heart swell with every note. After her was a band composed of four young men and a single girl, combining the beautiful, haunting notes of a violin and the steady support of the cello with metal-like melodies from the guitar and some real thrashing from the drums. It was an intense sort of juxtaposition, but Teddy found herself liking it. If only because it was her kids from her community finding a safe space to explore and perform.

She wasn't crying. She *wasn't.* If there were a few tears in her eyes by the time the last group came out to do an excerpt from *A Midsummer Night's Dream,* well that was just because it was dry in the gymnasium. Maybe she would ask Silas to get her a humidifier for Christmas.

When the final group marched off, then everyone came back for the curtain call, she was on her feet and applauding loudly. She wasn't the only one either. Aunties. Uncles. Grandmothers. Grandfathers. Tired moms who worked too hard, tired fathers with the weight of the world on their shoulders. Sisters who took care of their siblings when there wasn't anyone else to do so. Brothers who knew what it was like to step up and be the man of the house. Old. Young. Black. Hispanic. White. Immigrant. Citizen. All of them clapping for their children. Clapping for their future.

Okay, maybe Teddy was crying. Because how could she not? It was her community, her family, all able to celebrate the potential of their loved ones together. When she was a kid, she had dreamed of a place like the very one she was in. And now she had it. Now they *all* had it.

The cheering went on for a long while, some of the kids giggling, some of them waving. The older kids, meanwhile, were having stronger reactions. Some crying, some bowing repeatedly. She knew some of what they were going through, just a bit. She remembered what it was like to be young and poor and feel like the whole world was against them. Being appreciated for what they were, for what they could do, could do wonders for a growing soul.

Eventually, however, the cacophony did die down and she lowered herself into her seat. She picked up one of the deviled eggs that she had completely forgotten about during the show, finally nibbling at it.

"You know," she said, once she swallowed. "This was a test more than anything. Considering how well this went, I'm sure Mrs. Sanchez will be comfortable doing an actual play at the end of the summer. She said if there's enough interest from adults in the neighborhood, she would like to open casting to the whole community."

"That would be lovely, wouldn't it?" Mrs. Miller said.

But there was something off about her tone. Something near teary. Sure, Teddy was in near tears, her throat still narrow from all the emotion, but why would—

The lights, which had come up for the curtain call, dimmed to nearly being off. Alarmed, Teddy turned back to the stage to find there was a single person there, standing in the spotlight.

Silas.

"Hello, everyone," he said, his voice loud but with a slight tremor of nerves to it. What was he doing? "I'm sure all of you know this by now, but I wanted to recognize the woman who made this all happen. Without her, this community center never would have been built, and I would not have had the pleasure of getting to know this beautiful neighborhood and all of the wonderful people in it."

What was he doing?

He took a step off the stage and the light followed him, a shining beacon through the open space. Everyone was quiet, and Teddy swore each of them could hear the confused thundering of her heart.

"But there's more you should know. Ms. Teddy Parker didn't just encourage my family to invest in your town. She encouraged me to invest in *myself*. To open my eyes to all the potential I had to change the world. About the worth of community, and kindness. That there is more to life than a dollar sign.

"And I cannot tell you how much she had improved my life. Made it better. Better than any right it had to be." He was still walking toward her, and a chorus of awws sounded from all over. It had taken a while for the folks in her area to feel comfortable around Silas, and then the other Millers that would visit. But after a year and a half, they had managed to win a good number of the denizens over.

Especially the young ones, but that was probably because Silas always brought new toys and gadgets with him every time he stopped in at the community center.

"I don't know what my world would be like if Teddy hadn't popped into my life, armed with a baseball bat and ready to throw down for my honor—"

A titter from the others. Perhaps her baseball bat had grown into a bit of a legend. It wasn't her fault it was the easiest to grab method of defense that she'd had in her possession since her softball days of high school.

Silas continued, "But I know my world would be a darker place. An emptier place. Teddy is my light. She reminds me to be a better person. To do more. To *be* more. And most of all, to open myself up to all of the love and kindness that we can find in each other."

He reached her, and goodness if his gaze didn't still have the ability to take her breath away. "To *trust* each other."

And then he was kneeling, reaching into his pocket to pull out a little cobalt box that matched the curtains of the stage. With his thumb, he popped it open, and she was staring not at a diamond, but a beautiful jewel of amethyst.

Teddy hated diamonds. She thought they were plain, and it was only the shrewd hoarding of the De Vries family that made them valuable. She didn't like that people died for them either, enough to make 'blood diamonds' a common term. Her father always thought she was being dramatic every time she got on *that* particular soapbox, but apparently Silas had listened.

Because amethyst was her mother's birthstone. And amethyst was Teddy's favorite color. She didn't care much for jewelry, but the only necklace and bracelet she owned were both silver with amethyst accents.

Could he be any more perfect?

"Theodora Parker, will you marry me?"

So much flooded her, too much to single out and think about. But she could sort it later. All she had to worry about at the moment was saying yes.

"*Yes!*" she cried, nearly flinging herself into his lap. "Yes, absolutely, *yes*. Yes!"

She was laughing. She was also crying again. Maybe Silas was crying too. But that was alright because she was so happy that she might just burst at the seams. Somehow, he slid that ring onto her finger, and then they were kissing. Kissing while everyone cheered around them. Bringing hope for good things to come for the entire community.

Because, as far as the future Mrs. Teddy Parker-Miller was concerned, her future was full of more hope and possibility than she could ever imagine.

She couldn't wait.

HELLO READER! I hope you enjoyed Silas and Theodora's love story. Ready to read about the next brother up for love? Sterling Miller helps someone out who breaks down near their property and it's a good thing, because she's a veterinarian and they just so happen to be in need of a vet. He just doesn't expect her to be so blunt about the condition of the animals on the ranch. Elizabeth has no problem telling him like it is. I suppose you could say this is a bit of an enemies to lovers sweet romance.

You can find Sterling and Elizabeth's love story on all major retailers. However, I'd be more than happy if you chose to buy it from my own small online business. Scan the QR code below (or on the next page, depending on the formatting of this book) to be taken to In Debt to the Cowboy at Natalie Dean Books. If scanning QR codes isn't your thing, you can also find my store here: nataliedeanbooks.com

ABOUT THE AUTHOR

Born and raised in a small coastal town in the south, I was raised to treasure family and love the Lord. I'm a dedicated homeschooling mom who loves to travel and spend time with my growing-up-too-fast son.

When I'm not busy writing or running my business, you can find me cleaning house, cooking dinner, feeding our three rescue cats, trying to make learning fun and coaxing my son to pick up his toys. On less busy days, you may also find me paddling down a spring run in Florida, hiking a mountain trail in Georgia (on the rare vacation to the mountains), or enjoying a book.

If you love Natalie Dean books, you can be notified of new releases by signing up to my newsletter at nataliedeanau thor.com, where you will also receive two free short stories for signing up. Just click on the "Free Books" tab at the top and you'll be on your way!

Also, as previously mentioned, I've opened my own online bookstore and I'd love your support! As of June 2024, I'm selling my ebooks at Natalie Dean Books. By late summer or fall 2024, I should have audiobooks, regular paperbacks, large print paperbacks, dyslexic print paperbacks and signed paperbacks all available. At the request of my loyal readers, I'll also be adding merchandise, such as glasses, cups, magnets and more. So come check out my small mom-owned author business at nataliedeanbooks.com.

You can also scan the QR code below to be taken to the home page of Natalie Dean Books.

facebook.com/nataliedeanromance

www.ingramcontent.com/pod-product-compliance
Lightning Source LLC
Chambersburg PA
CBHW061125310726

48974CB00002B/683